I0592901

The Draper Diaries

Revised Edition

Gregory Round

Remember, remember the fifth of November, the gunpowder, treason and plot. I know of no reason why gunpowder treason should ever be forgot.
Anon.

To the memory of those Cold War combatants who lost their lives in space programs.

Thanks to:
Gabriella "Biella" Coleman for permission to use an excerpt from her book "What It's Like to Participate in Anonymous' Actions"

Prologue

Within this novel you will see some formatting that may seem unfamiliar. The speech method used is more like a movie script than a regular novel. I use a character's name or initials in grey to introduce speech. This enables the reader to see the character's name as a background word and makes reading the dialogue easier than if I followed the usual practices.

When a quote is given from a third party source (yes I have quoted in a fiction book) I begin the quote with [name] (name being the person or website where the information came from) and end the quote with [name]. If there is more than one quote from the same source or author, a number will appear after the end quote. If I have paraphrased or, in the case of a Wikipedia article, edited and changed, then only the end quote will appear after the sentence or paragraph. References can be found at the back of the book

The quotes are used in a seamless way, and colored grey, to enable them to flow with the story and not be a side issue. I call this method, 'The Flow Method'.

Also, within the story you will see the word clue, this means that you should remember that particular clue, so you can decipher the ending of the story.

Gregory J Round
2017 and 2025

Part One: Misdirection

INTRODUCTION

NEWS FLASH: THE NATIONAL SEDA BUILDING LONGREACH, IN VERONA, NEW JERSEY, HAS BEEN BOMBED. FORTY ONE LIVES HAVE BEEN LOST AND HUNDREDS INJURED. MORE TO FOLLOW AS SOON AS IT COMES TO HAND.

On July 16th 2017, the online hacktivist group Anonymous, hacked into the Space Exploration and Development Agency's (SEDA) website. They left a message stating that they had evidence of a murderous plot carried out by the SEDA space agency in the 1960s. Their message disclosed the existence of a set of journals that had been found by an undisclosed source and that these journals were then digitized and stored remotely. Anonymous named these journals The Draper Diariess, in remembrance of Charlie Draper, the first man to walk on the moon and his crew, Ed Robertson and Aaron Rosenbach. The information within the Diaries threatens to destroy and shame the achievements of the 1960s space program and expose the lies and corruption of the SEDA. There were several demands;

Free Bradley Manning, drop all actions against Julian Assange (including the false rape charges), forgive Edward Snowden and tell the world how it was duped in regards to the Athena Moon Mission deaths.

In 1967, SEDA sent three astronauts on a journey to the Moon. The space agency shared a goal with the Government, to reach the Moon with a manned mission before the USSR. There was a secondary reason (if not the main reason) for the space race. Economically, both the USSR and the USA were struggling. Even though the future 'looked' bright, at least for the US, secret analysis revealed a massive drop in economic growth in the near future. Only an extended fiscal program would save the nation. Wars, usually do this. It is war that drives industry and promotes economic recovery. However, wars can also destroy local, social cohesion, escalating and festering community complaints from a blurred background to a prominent spatial dilema. Left unchecked, the focus on war shifts our gaze from immediate concerns to distant futurisms. Sneaking up from the shadows, poverty, derived from inflation, can breed the type of dissent that is far more dangerous than shaking the hands of an enemies ideology. Relevant Soviet Ministers and US officials, agreed to create and maintain a space race, which would include misdirection, for the benefit of both nations. The Russians needed US wheat as their stranglehold on Ukraine's primary industries was not enough to feed the Russian masses within the wider USSR. The USA needed foreign funding that could be used for scientific purposes. Both nations would rely on each other's silence and economically, they both needed each other in a symbiotic relationship, whilst still showing the world that they were manifestly in opposition to each others political and social views.

The US and the Soviets were engaged in a proxy war in Vietnam, and both sides continued the threat to each other of nuclear annihilation: although this was just a game. The worlds political power is really run by economic giants that give 'power' to a few, like the tailor gave the king his new clothes. Naked in truth and delusional in power.

This book tells the stories of the Astronaut patriots and the Anonymous heroes, caught up in a surrealist world of ideological and economic machinations. It tells of the fracturing of their lives, the sorrow brought to their families and the misdirection performed by SEDA and the USSR, in front of the entire world. It reveals secret links between the KGB and SEDA's Space Agency Security Services (SASS), exposing damning evidence from both sides.

My name is Virgil Kaine, and this is a true story. I am writing this in self-imposed exile from a secret location. I am wanted by SASS and the FBI. The Russians also would like a piece of me. Two of my friends have been murdered. The National SEDA building Longreach, in Verona, New Jersey, has been bombed. Forty one lives have been lost and hundreds injured. The activist group Anonymous and I have been blamed for this terrorist act. I did not commit these crimes. I have been Diariesing Anonymous' findings from The Draper Diariess on the Truth's News website. Much has been uncovered and much will be difficult to believe. [Wintzer]For this was the age of great secrets [Wintzer 2017].

Virgil

It was a typically cold winter's day. New York had been very good to me financially and personally, although I struggled with the differences in the seasonal climate. Born in Broken Hill, New South Wales, Australia, you would think that I was use to such climatic differences. After-all, Broken Hill can reach the high 40s (Celsius) in summer and be freezing in winter. But walking among the concrete trees and their shadows in NYC was different to the open horizons of the Outback. I loved both life styles. NYC was clean, tall and powerful. The Outback was dusty, red and unkind to those that disrespected it. A place suited to outlaws[1].

I was living with the beautiful Cara Lucas, my long-term girlfriend and soul mate. Cara and I were working in opposite fields. I was a journalist with the New York Truth Online News Agency and Cara, was a field agent for the FBI. That's not to infer that the FBI lies. Rather it shows the difference in methodologies used by the two systems. The FBI retains information that they consider is not for public release, and the Truth, well, we release everything.

Occasionally there were flash points of opinion, between Cara and I, however, we survived each time and reconciliation was always warmly received. At times I thought the clashes were implemented just for the result. Does reconciliation and all that it brings, become a habit, or an addiction? Her work meant a lot to her and often had her away on 'secret missions' for many days. It was not

---

1   Clue

unusual to not hear from her for up to a week. But hey, that's her job.

We lived in a quintessential big apple apartment on the third floor. Facing the street are three windows. Two of these windows had access to a metal fire escape. The building's facade was painted white with gold trim. It looked out of place with our Spartan interior. A sofa, small table, plastic dining table, well, I called it a dining table, and a tall bookcase loaded with newspapers, old books and manuscripts. Beneath ground level was a basement designed and configured for a family of giant rabbits. There were rooms, anterooms, half repaired masonry nooks and tight passageways between support walls. Spiders loved to spin their homes down there. We had a small cupboard in the disused janitor's room and an even smaller table with a plastic garden chair. Mostly no other occupants visited the Rabbit Warren, as we called it, and I found it a sanctuary when I was on an article deadline. Cara despised the place, she was and arachnophobic totally refused to go there. She couldn't get my cell phone when I was in the Warren, as there was no coverage. So if I wasn't at home and I couldn't be raised, I was most likely with the spiders.

I was alerted to the hacking of the SEDA website by my editor, Hugo Kent. He wanted a quick response as it was the 50th anniversary of the first moon landing. Online news is a case of the quick or the unread. There is no time for contemplation, articles must be written quickly and succinctly. I surfed to SEDA's website and found it was down. No web pages no story. I knew that a copy would be in Google's servers, so I clicked the arrow sign near the

Google search result URL for SEDA and retrieved a cached version. The page had a photo of a person wearing an Anonymous mask with the message: We are Legion. We do not forget. We do not forgive. Expect Us! A second message had their demands. It was clear after looking at the site that these guys were about to unleash another of their now infamous campaigns.

I needed to find out more about these hacktivist so I had to do some digging. I found that Anonymous has no defined philosophy. Internal dissidence is a regular feature of the group. A website associated with them describes it as 'an Internet gathering' with 'a very loose and decentralized command structure, which operates on ideas rather than directives.' [Coleman]In some ways, it may be impossible to gauge the intent and motive of thousands of participants, many of whom don't even bother to leave a trace of their thoughts, motivations, and reactions. Among those that do, opinions vary considerably. [Coleman]

[Wikipedia]Broadly speaking, Anons oppose Internet censorship and control, and the majority of their actions target governments, organizations, and corporations that they accuse of censorship. Anons were early supporters of the global Occupy movement and the Arab Spring. [Wikipedia: 1]

This was a news worthy story, as SEDA isn't hacked every day, well, never really. I couldn't see any of their demands being met and I guessed, that wasn't the point. Anonymous are more about exposing government secrets to the world rather than demanding prisoners be released; that's a job for Amnesty International. So I expected more fun to follow, as they say in the classics. It was time to write my article on the first Moon landing. In doing so I wanted to get in touch with the Anonymous movement. If indeed the Anons had serious damning evidence about the Athena Moon Mission, then the Truth wanted exclusivity.

The Truth News Online

July 17 2017

Fifty Years of Dreams

By Virgil Kaine

"On the 19th of July 1967 a small disheveled looking spacecraft named the Lewis, piloted by Charlie Draper and Edward Robinson, had its descent engine throttled back on the journey toward the surface of the moon. The two astronauts inside, standing at their respective controls, could not see the surface well enough to make the descent to a soft landing. At this stage, the descent was controlled by the inboard computer. That computer has less computing power than an early model mobile phone. The astronauts were able to manipulate the rocket engine's thrust only. To land, they had to slowly reduce the thrust enough to counter the Moon's 1/6th Earth gravity. This was a difficult maneuver, and it relied on the skill of these two fighter-jet test pilots. One mistake, and they would plunge to their certain deaths. When they saw the onrushing target area, both realized that they were heading for an impact crater with a very rocky ejector field. The ejector field is a result of the blast caused by a meteor impact, it throws rocks and dust out in a wide radius of ground zero. With their adrenaline surging and hearts racing, instead of continuing down, Charlie Draper, the command pilot, flicked the autopilot to off and grabbed the directional controls.

Draper did not ask permission for the change of plan as he knew that time was critical and the transmissions to and fro from the Moon to Earth were often delayed or full of static. An impact was imminent if they did nothing. The ground control crew, 250,000 miles away, heard only the voice of Ed Robinson as he was reading the numbers from the instruments panel. 'Hang on we are go. 2,000 feet.' Longreach Control showed the altitude dropping 1,600 feet, 1,400, 1,000. The computer flashed a warning 1202. The two moon men said nothing. Not until the Lewis reached 750 feet did Robertson speak again, '750, coming down at 23, 600 feet, down at 19, 540 feet, down at 15, 400 feet, down at 9, 8 feet per second, forward, 330, 3½ down.' The Lewis was braking its fall, as it should, and moving slowly forward. But now Longreach realized that something was wrong. The Athena lander had almost stopped dropping, and suddenly, between 300 and 200 feet its port yaw thrusters fired and quickly increased the speed from 16 feet per second to 80 feet per second, roughly 55 miles an hour! This was an unrehearsed move and caught everyone at Longreach by surprise. As the forward speed reduced the Lander's downward drop, the velocity increased slightly.

'Down at 2½, 19 forward, 3½ down, 220 feet, 11 forward, coming down nicely, 200 feet, 4½ down, 160, 6½ down, 9 forward 100 feet.' Then, surprisingly, a red light flashed on the Lewis' instrument panel, warning Mission Control that they had a problem. The flight controllers knew what was wrong, the inboard computer was overloaded and there may have been a brake in one of its rope memory modules. The lander only had 5 percent of descent fuel remaining. According to agreed protocol, the Lewis must be on the surface within 94 seconds, or the crew must abort the mission to land on the moon. But this mission was never going backwards the crew were determined to land.

To abort, they would have to push the descent engine's controls up to full throttle and ignite the ascent engine to get enough power to brake the connections with the decent module and the moon's gravitational tug, and speed back into Lunar orbit, for a rendezvous with the Command and Service module, the Santa Maria. At the 60 seconds mark the countdown began. "Sixty seconds" called Astronaut David Spitzer, the capsule communicator or CapCom, as they were called at Longreach. With sixty seconds to go, every man in the control center held his breath.

CapCom was remembering a comment made by Charlie when he said during a launch test only a few months ago, 'how are we going to get to the moon if we can't even get off the launch pad'. The comment reverberated through his mind. The 60 seconds seemed like a lifetime. Congress would withdraw funding if the Mission failed. That would lead to national and international shame. Now, was all to be lost for the sake of a few seconds of fuel?

'Lights on!' Robertson confirmed he had seen the fuel warning light. "Down 2½" Robertson continued. 'Forward, forward. Good, 40 feet, down 2½. Picking up some dust. 30 feet. 2½ down. Faint shadow.' He had seen the shadow of one of the 68-inch probes extending from Lewis' foot pads. When these probes touch the ground they signaled to the pilot, via the instrument panel, to shut down the rocket engine.

'Four forward, drifting to the right a little.' "Thirty seconds," announced CapCom. Thirty seconds: to live or die! In the control center you could hear the silence as every person was glued to their respective readouts and listening to the transmission.

"Forward, drifting right," Robertson said. With less than 20 seconds of descent engine fuel left, came the highly anticipated words: 'Contact light!' The landing probes had touched the surface.

A moment or two later Robertson was heard to say, "Engine shutdown." After a long pause the now famous words from Draper were transmitted, "Longreach, Grissom Base here. The Lewis has made touchdown." [Wikipedia. 2]

Great discoveries were made and new horizons crossed, as science progressed due to the work of these and other brave astronauts. Men and women who challenged the notion of defeat and gave victory instead. Now 50 years on we know the result. A tragic set of events that destroyed the lives of so many people. Ed Robertson and Aaron Rosenbach joined Charlie Draper in their infamous fiery plunge to their deaths.

In the remembrance of heroic deeds we sometimes forget sub plots that secretly change events. Actors brace themselves against the wind of deceit, to give, as magicians, the greatest misdirection in human history.

Today Anonymous has spoken to the world. They say that they have some evidence that will ruin the 1960s space race achievements and expose a massive fraud: even MURDER.

What evidence? In connection with whom? I am ready to discuss this with any Anon that has this information. As Anonymous suggest, your identity will remain hidden. I don't even have to meet you in person. You can send some of this damning evidence to my phone. The Truth will help!"

Hugo got a called from none other than the SEDA Director that same day. She wanted to appeal to him to stop any articles about the Athena missions from gaining momentum. "This was a year to remember those lost and to celebrate their achievements, not spread lies", she told him. I knew that Hugo would not follow such a direction even if it came from the President of the USA himself. 'The press is a free agent' he would always say and 'protected by the 1st amendment' I would reply. Rosealee Mishin was pushing the proverbial up hill. We were on to something big and nothing was going to get in our way. Well, at least that's what I thought at the time.

It's not to be unexpected that when things go wrong they hit the fan in a big way. Athena was like, 'winning one for the Gippa' as far as the Gold War was concerned. The US had to be seen to be in front and winning the game. Later that day, while riding the Tube, I received a call from a mystery woman. She wanted to meet: no name given. I asked where and when and how was I going to recognize her. She said she would approach me as I was known. Was she with Anonymous? That's hard to determine unless she admits she is. Before I could pry any further, she terminated the call. I guess cell phones are a trap for those who aren't extra careful.

I have always believed in the true values of the great nation of the USA. Freedom of the press is a constitutional guarantee and must never be compromised by thought or favor, and after becoming a citizen of the US I aimed to protect the values found in that constitution. My desires to tell the truth led me to work for a news agency with the same name as my desires: funny that. It was a career that I believed in and gave my life to. Any event that required an accurate and critical Diaries, landed on my desk. I covered the United States Holocaust Memorial Museum shooting, when in June 2009, an elderly white supremacist James von Brunn, who had attempted to kidnap Federal Reserve employees in 1981, shot and killed a police officer at the United States Holocaust Museum, before being wounded by first respondents. The 2009 Fort Hood shootings, Nidal Malik Hasan, a US Army Major serving as a Psychiatrist, killed 13 military personnel and wounded 29 at Fort Hood, Texas. The Pentagon shooting, where John Patrick Bedell shot and wounded two Pentagon police officers, at a security checkpoint in the Pentagon station. The Times Square car bombing attempt. When a bomb ignited by Faisal Shahzad in Times Square failed to explode. He was later captured attempting to flee the country.

The Portland car bomb plot when Mohamud Osman Mohamud, born in Somalia, attempted to set off what he thought was a car bomb at a Christmas tree lighting ceremony in Portland, Oregon. After his death sentence was overturned, he was sentenced to thirty years imprisonment. Had he taken the lives of innocent children and their parents, enjoying the true values of living in the US, what would have been said?

Several people who wanted him dead no matter what, confronted me and wanted me to Diaries their concerns. They wanted all people of Muslim background deported from US soil. Their reasoning was that, here was a man who their country decided to help. To give him a new life with opportunity and security, and he repaid that charity and trust by trying to murder and maim US citizens. I wrote in an article the next day that it was time to think about suspending refugee immigration, until such a time, when global tensions were more at rest. Although I never published the complete desires of those who came to me, as that would be unethical and unrealistic. After-all, there are 3.45 Million Muslims in the US and the majority are law abiding people. All the acts of terrorism were perpetrated by those who did not share our values. They were the enemy from within, and we must remain vigilant because there will be many more to come. However, my most dangerous story yet, has been covering the sudden Athena revelations from Anonymous.

I met 'mystery woman' at Battery Park near the Alberti Marker. She was somewhat nervous and twitchy. I asked her for her name. She said, "names are not important at this stage, only the truth is important." I told her I was cutting it fine for a meeting with Hugo, a man that lived for deadlines and punctuality. Even though I called him a friend, on work matters he was not to be pissed off by bad time management, so we needed to get this done: trying not to be abrupt. She didn't want to sit and talk, giving no reason really, so we walked. Mystery woman was of medium build, dark hair, brown eyes and an uneasy look about her. I decided there and then that she needed a code name. Looking out across the water I saw the statue of Liberty, so I called her Liberty Belle, after-all, she was gorgeous and we were discussing liberty: I think?
Whenever I am in Lower Manhattan, I always ponder over the lives lost in the World Trade Center. No liberty there. I was 22 at the time. It shaped my life forever. Once those great tombstones of power cast their shadows over the

heart of the free world. Now a silent painful memory, yet I still see them.

Liberty Belle (LB) said she knows some members of Anonymous and they want to talk to me, however, security is of paramount concern. Me: Are you an Anon? LB: 'No.' Me: 'Well what do they have?' She looked at me still trying to determine if I was indeed on their side. LB: 'More than SEDA wants the world to hear, Mr. Virgil.' That was enough to get me interested, so a meeting was arranged via a chat site, on the Deep Web.

All contacts would be done behind VPN (Virtual Private Network) giving the best encrypted security. LB was going to introduce me to the notorious Anon: Revenge (or so she said) he was known as REV. REV was on the countries most wanted list. He had hacked into many government sites and has been releasing government data at will. Every law enforcement agency in the US wanted to get rid of Anon: Revenge.

LB gave me a cheat sheet showing how to setup a VPN account on the Deep Web. As if I didn't know how. She was very cautious and was constantly looking over her shoulders. We ended up near the Control Station underground entrance. LB: 'It looks like a mausoleum, don't you think?' Me: 'What does?' LB: 'The Control Station.' Me: 'Never saw it like that before, but yeah I guess it does.' Whether it did look like a tomb or not, it was a good exit point for both of us to use. A quick handshake and we made our own way out of there.

I arrived back at the office just short of the scheduled meeting time, giving Hugo the news about an up and coming meeting with Anonymous. Hugo: 'Can we trust the authenticity of these leaks? I may have to put my head on a chopping block here, but I will do that if we can uncover a massive story, that's even bigger than Woodward and Bernstein's.' Every editor wants a Pulitzer Prize. Me: 'May as well go with it Hugo. What have we got to lose?' Hugo: 'Our freedom.'

Hugo was concerned that if we published fake news it would seriously harm the Truth's reputation. I understood his line of thought, but to get a story on the old school space program, and that story be a revelation, is a chance I couldn't miss out on.

 I left and headed home to setup my VPN as instructed. It took me longer than I thought. These Anon guys must be at it 24/7 to be able to achieve anything. I logged into the chosen chat room using an onion browser, with the Anon, Hermes, and found Anon: Revenge. That was easy! Or did he find me? Anon: Revenge; Hermes, the info we want you to print is at a drop point in Kumlau Square in China Town, now known as DP #1. Be there today at 1300hrs. You will have to decipher some of the information. There will be an app to do that. Anon: Hermes; OK. Who will meet me? Anon: Revenge; You will be contacted. You are known. We are Legion! doN't fUck uP!

I wasn't intending to do anything of the kind. This Anon could be a kid still in high school or a freshman at college and he's telling me a 38 year old leading journo not to fuck up! Damn his pimples!

I tracked my way to drop point #1, Kumlau Square in China Town, via a Yellow. I could see a woman sitting on a seat across from the Asian Bank building. She was wearing a hoodie and her face was in shadow. Everything about her suggested contact, or was that my self-induced pickup line. She stood up when she saw me approaching but never quite looked at me directly. Good peripherals I remember saying to myself. She left a memory stick on the seat. I sat down and covered it with my leg. Thinking, good pins as well, as she walked away. My fly-by- night contact, was average height. Jeans and t-shirt was her fashion choice for this day. Maybe that was her fashion thing. Putting the memory stick into my right side pocket, I stood and nervously moved on. All the way back home I was wondering if anyone was following me. I didn't want to go back to the office, as there were too many prying eyes. Text from Hugo: 'Any luck yet Verge?' Me: 'On way home to decipher.' Hugo: 'Ring me when ready.'

Back at the ranch (a name Cara and I gave our sprawling almost empty home), I put the memory stick into my laptop. What I saw was a large folder hierarchy with names like; oppression, cover up, debate, moon shine, SEDA, SASS, USSR, and a lot more. This was going to be a long afternoon. There was a great deal of information to digest. At first, I couldn't get my head around the chaos of it all. But later I set out making more folders and dropping different documents into them. Most of these Anons are people that really don't care about the structure of a filing system. They just like to hack them. A Journalist needs to have a well-organized desktop, whether that be hardwood or digital.

I read Diariess on the moon landings, in particular the Athena program. Others were details of construction failures and financial rip-offs. The information was so damning that I kind of wondered, if I was caught with this time bomb, I may end up in the American equivalent of a Russian gulag, Guantanamo!

Hugo said to upload my article ASAP and we would wait for a reaction. Any reaction was good publicity for the Truth and publicity equaled income, and Hugo if nothing else, was a company man.

The Truth News Online

July 18 2017

Smoke and Mirrors

By Virgil Kaine

"Following on from my article last week on the 50th anniversary of the Athena moon landing, and after many complaints from various sources, my editor has kindly allowed me to expand on what I said in the last paragraph. Here is a refresher of that paragraph.
'Great discoveries were made and new horizons crossed as science progressed due to the work of these and other brave astronauts. Men and women who challenged the notion of defeat and gave victory instead. Now 50 years on, we know the result. A tragic set of events that destroyed the lives of so many people. Ed Robertson and Aaron Rosenbach joined Charlie Draper in a fiery plunge to their deaths. In the remembrance of heroic deeds, we sometimes forget sub plots that secretly change events. Actors brace themselves against the wind of deceit, to give, as magicians, the greatest misdirection in human history.'

I have been asked to explain what I meant by the greatest misdirection in human history. Everyone knows the official story of Athena. The US space agency, SEDA, lands a manned space craft successfully on the surface of the moon at Mare Grissom [Clue]. This was a great human feat (even though three men died doing it) and the entire world rejoiced in their success. Well, maybe not the Soviets. It was of paramount importance that we, 'the free world leader', had to defeat the 'evildoers' wanting to destroy our way of life.

Many people are skeptical of this achievement. Many others live in the glory of its being. The one absolute in this discourse is to understand what you are defending or not defending. SEDA has told the world that the three astronauts, Charlie Drake, Ed Robertson and Aaron Rosenbach, tragically died on re-entry to the earth's atmosphere when their command module's heat shield malfunctioned.

It was believed that a rogue Russian satellite smashed into the command module and tore its heat shield off. This led to the capsule plunging through the atmosphere at 20,000 kilometers per hour, heating up to 6000 degrees and smashing into the northern terminus of the Appalachian Trail, on Mt. Katahdin. The human remains found, were fused onto and in some cases, into, plastic and metal from the spaceship interior. It must have been hell for the families to know that, and they faced it in public at Arlington, with great courage.

There was a worldwide broadcast of the funeral and every government building and many private business' had their flags at half-mast. Later the a story was leaked to the media about a Russian rogue satellite that went off course and hit the Santa Maria, dislodging her heat shield. The heat shield protects the astronauts from the atmospheric friction.

Inevitably, there were those that expanded the story to outright Soviet murder. There were protest marches and even some embassies around the globe were attacked with rocks and small fire bombs. Both the US Government and the Soviet Government had to call for calm. The Soviets were furious at the claims and Diariess are widely known, albeit not substantiated, that they, the Soviets, aided North Vietnam to create the 1968 chiếm lại offensive, an escalation of the Vietnam war that almost gave victory to the North, in retaliation for the accusations leveled at them. Today I can Diaries that much of the official Moon story is a lie. However, the moon landing did take place. The deaths of the astronauts did happen, just not in the way that history now tells us."

Over the coming weeks the Truth will be publishing a series of compelling articles that will not only embarrass SEDA, but also condemn their actions. I am in the possession of a set of journals from anonymous sources, loosely called The Draper Diaries.
The Draper Diaries is packed with important information that not only criticizes the space program, but also, condemns actions taken in the name of national security. Each day I will release a small section of these Diariess. Each release will have clues as to what took place in 1967. A conclusion will not be given. Because of legal requirements, the Truth must remain impartial. However, you the readers of these articles can gather the facts, and the clues, then come to your own conclusions. These Diaries are going to be bigger than WikiLeaks ever was. The first release will be tomorrows afternoon's edition on our website.

The first drop of Draper ink that I decided to publish, was a Morse Code message, recorded by Alfonso Cipriani (an Italian PhD student) in 1967, from deep space: beyond the moon. Cipriani saw this remarkable message as a crude trick in light of the Athena moon landing that was underway at the time of the transmission. Even though Cipriani tested the telemetry and it showed an origin from beyond the moon, he believed it may have been the Russians playing a game, at the expense of the US space program, after all, he was watching the daily news Diariess from the moon. How could anyone fake that, right? Not playing it for anyone else (due to his desire to succeed in graduate school), he filed it away on a computer server at the Università degli Studi di Milano. UNIX network address 172.31.39.125 password unknown.

The Truth News Online

July 19 2017

SOS from Beyond the Moon

By Virgil Kaine

"Today I am releasing a mystery from outer-space. A message received by a lone amateur radio enthusiast, Alfonso Cipriani, in July 1967. This was not a voice message, but an SOS in Morse code.
Morse Code Message
'SOS to the world SOS they have murdered me.'
Was this message for real? Did Cipriani discover a massive disaster in the Athena space program? Or, was this a cheap hoax by someone with advanced radio transmission skills.

Could a message in Morse code be transmitted from somewhere on the Earth, and bounced back to the Earth, to give the false impression that an astronaut, or cosmonaut, was in trouble? You the reader must retain this and every other clue, for the final article published here on the Truth website, will be the cipher required to connect all the dots."

That is as far as the article went. It was online Friday at 5.30PM. The shit hit the fan at 5.46PM. So do you think someone was watching us? Hugo got a call from a Guy Southerby, saying he represented the NSA. Southerby demanded that the Truth cease and desist from publishing unsubstantiated material designed to erode the people's confidence in Government achievements. He told Hugo that, 'this is a new methodology of terrorist organizations. They attempt to subvert the very ethos of their target nation', and that, we are all responsible to protect the beliefs and achievements of the USA.' I was questioning what this had to do with the NSA. It's more a matter for the FBI, I would have thought.

To say that Hugo was not happy, would be like saying you were served warm casket wine in a posh restaurant and charged for ROMANEE CONTI '54. Hugo slammed the phone down and picked up some papers off his desk, shuffling and staking them as he told me, 'he was never going to be bullied by anyone let alone some pretentious upstart from the government'. He was visibly shaking when my cell phone rang. When I left the office, I noticed a dark van just up the street. It looked out of place and I guessed it would be this Sotherby's goons [clue]. If indeed he was who he said he was and if he had goons. A moot point really.

The call came in from LB, asking me to attend a function at the Russian Consulate at 91st Street. Why would she want me to attend such a thing and who was she? I must admit I was very intrigued so I accepted. Knowing that Cara was on duty somewhere, I didn't send a message.

The Consulate was lit up like Christmas and people looked like they were flowing in along some long river of delusion. LB introduced me to Vasily Khovanski, a top level diplomat visiting the embassy from Russia. She somehow avoided saying her name. That bugged me but this was not the place to question her about her identity. Khovanski was somewhat loud to be a diplomat and he slurped his vodka. The idea was, that he get to know me a little, then question me about The Draper Diaries. That's what I assumed anyway.

I was mentally shaking my head and trying to work out, what The Draper Diaries had to do with the Russians. Apparently, in 1961 the USSR space program had a few disasters that were not made public: as if we didn't know that. However, a CIA agent in Lisbon taped a conversation between the Soviets and a female astronaut in low earth orbit. Her name was Alexandrina Yeltsin, the first human *unofficially* in space. Charlie Draper had the ear of some CIA operatives who told him about the Lisbon recording. So Draper typed up an account of the tail on a SEDA mainframe.

The story goes that Yeltsin, was used as a guinea pig to test a new guidance system. The guidance system failed and sent her towards a steep re-entry. Her cries for help, her voice in fear and the cold hardhearted ground control reply, would have shocked the world and expose the old Soviet Union, as a callus cold blooded killer of its own heroes, if it ever got out. Moreover, the US government would be questioned by its constituents about the safety of our space program. Khovanski: 'I am telling you this Mr. Virgil, because I know you have the incident in the so called Draper Diaries. So let's be honest and open with each other. Both our countries will be in, how do you say, deep shit if this gets out.' Was this the SOS recorded by Cipriani, the Morse code cry of help from a woman facing her death in deep space?

Khovanski explained that the SASS (Space Agency Security Service) knows about that incident and a number of others that could potentially rewrite the course of history. Therefore, if I exposed SEDA then SASS would leak the Soviet disasters. He said that SASS would believe that my actions, in publishing any of the diary entries, would be as a result of the control of past KGB operatives. And that, these operatives are disillusioned with modern Russia and determined to resurrect the Cold War. Of course that would start an avalanche of secret reveals and return both countries to the pre-detente era. He explained that the repercussions for both countries and the multitude of world conflicts that would result from this knowledge, would be disastrous. I saw this as more of a threat than a reality. But who am I to know what goes on in the dark secret world of cross government activities. Maybe it would plunge the world into a recession, or even a war! The decision to make was obvious.

Fuck the Russians and stuff SEDA!

Text message from Cara: 'See me urgently.' This was unlike Cara to send a message like that. Maybe something was going down at work and she thought there could be a story in it for the Truth. Or maybe my mine was rambling again. Something that is a constant problem for me. We met at Sarabeth's on Madison, a great place for brunch & dessert, no really, I mean it!

Cara: 'You are in deep shit V if the Bureau or the CIA get wind of that covert conversation in the consulate just now, all hell will brake loose. Someone will have to go, someone will have to be a scapegoat, and that someone may well be me. So please stay clear of international politics. For both our sake's.' Me: 'Oh, shit. I didn't know you would be there babe.' Cara: 'Doesn't matter if I was there or not, someone would be listening. You must be careful V when dealing with foreign governments.'

She had been on duty monitoring the Russians and heard the conversation. Deciding to record over the voice data and replacing it with older recorded material from the consulate, put her in a dangerous position. I should have told her where I was going. I fucked up.

Cara explained that the Bureau was already questioning her about me and that 'she should think of her career and end the relationship'. That's not the way to do business with Cara. In the two years we had known each other I found her to be strong willed and exceedingly loyal. However, I felt bad about getting in her way and wondered if I should ask her to leave for her own safety, at least until all this was over. When I suggested it; Cara: 'What! Are you playing for another reconciliation V?' There was something so beautiful about her when she had that half serious half playful look. Me: 'It's always a possibility.' The smiles gave way to concern as Cara spotted one of her colleagues across the room. Strange thing that, two FBI agents at the famous Sarabeth's, so far from FBI HQ. Maybe he was enjoying the food also, or, maybe he was tailing me or Cara, or both.

Cara

I knew they would be about somewhere, but really, outside our apartment, in plain sight: In a big black van. Men in shades even though it was dark. I looked at them just long enough for my eyes to adjust to the distance and the dark interior of the van. It was a Mexican stand-off of some type for just a few seconds. Cara grabbed my shirt from behind and coaxed me inside. They were not FBI, otherwise Cara would know them. We poured a drink and sat on the sofa. I turned on the TV with mute. We discussed what was happening and how we were going to get through it. These Anons were going to turn our lives upside down. The more we released the more trouble would come our way.

Cara: 'V, if you continue with this Anonymous campaign, I am going to be in a tight situation.' Me: 'Sure I realize that, but what else can I do?' Cara:, with some thought: 'Maybe you could freelance it to another network?' Me: 'That would be over Hugo's dead body.'

The main problem for Cara was her position with the FBI. She was going to be placed under serious stress as I published more from The Draper Diaries. Cara knew that SEDA would bring their security arm into the game eventually if I released too much. But what is too much? And SASS may already be on the job. She hadn't met any of the SASS operatives. However, she was told that they were so well protected, that no other agency was going to push them around. The SASS was America's version of the KGB: and some.

Cara had long beautiful blonde hair with bright clear blue eyes. The flicking blue TV glow highlighted her face. A slim girl that packed a vicious kick. She was a kick boxing champion. She loved her career, but at times, believed the bureau crossed the line into CIA territory. Her slim figure and gorgeous looks made her a target for any weirdos that she may be investigating. I worried about that, as anyone would, but I never said anything, because Cara was a modern woman and I was a modern man, well, mostly I was. She loved Jazz and was a keen roller derby player. That was excessively physical for me but I loved watching her do her stuff.

We met two years ago when I was covering an FBI media release. She was on duty as a minder for a Deputy Director. We caught each other's eye and had a mini train-commuter's romance. You know the type, when you are traveling on the tube and your eyes meet with another passengers. Nothing is said, but if it's a regular journey, you find yourself almost hoping that your commuting partner is on the train each day: morning and afternoon. Later that same day I received a text message from her asking to meet. I didn't know who this Cara was at the time, so like all journos looking for a story I obliged. And, as they say in the classics, the rest is history.

She was forthright in her approach to her work and at times could get herself into a state. Yes, she carried the job home with her when it became tough. But hey, I listened and often used some of the bits and bobs in my articles, without divulging too much.

After some discussions, we decided that the main issue at hand, for the Truth, myself and her, was The Draper Diaries and not any hoax allegations. SEDA couldn't care less if they were accused of faking it, after-all that always gave them a chance to keep their achievement alive and current. What they didn't like was my inference in the first article.

Misdirection meant more to them than just some-one saying the word hoax. Misdirection is a form of deception in which the attention of an audience (namely the world) is focused on one thing (a TV broadcast) in order to distract its attention from another (the Moon tragedy). Managing an audience's attention is the aim of all magicians and it was the foremost task of SASS. They also didn't know what else I had. There may be many other cover-ups of wrong doings, which would either embarrass past employees and politicians, or, bring criminal charges. There is not a person alive that wouldn't do anything to fight for their personal freedom.

Cara was investigating an enemy operative named Malina and didn't want the Anons story to get in her way. Fair enough I guess. This Malina woman entered the US illegally from Mexico. It was believed that she was a Russian Cyber terrorist working in the US on a Live OP. Cara explained that Live OPs meant the terrorist was on a mission, and most likely was going to create death and havoc, before slipping back over the border. It was Cara's job to track her down and find out what she was up to. Whilst this type of work would not have caused her any concern in the past, the opening of the Anon Cyber door was just too much of a coincidence and she saw it as a threat. We agreed to disagree, but I could see it was an issue for her.

To date, we have a secret woman LB, contact me and set me up to talk to Anon: REV, a wanted man, kid, girl or woman. Then LB asked me to attend a party at the Russian Consulate where I meet Khovanski. He spins me a line and hopes I fall for it. Now I find out that Cara is seeking a possible Russian spy with links to organized crime. I am intrigued as to what other machinations are about to unfold. As a journalist I couldn't wait, but as a partner to Cara I was concerned for her state of mind, her safety and our relationship.

Cell phone call from Hugo: 'Virgil there is an injunction on the Truth to pull your stories and not to publish anymore.' Me: 'So what are we doing?' Hugo: 'Legals are filing a defense using first amendment, they say it should easily over rule the injunction.' Me: 'Well let's get another slice of pie out of the fridge and share it around.' Hugo agreed and I set about writing the next column. Cara needed some space so I retired to the Warren.

The Truth News Online

July 20 2017

Athena this is Longreach over

By Virgil Kaine

VHF moon radio signal recorded in Australia (part thereof) July 22nd 1967. 'Lewis, this is Longreach over…Athena, Athena this is Longreach, do you copy?…(static noises, gravelly……broken…………voice)…Say…
again……..Lewis……………
Longreach…….we…..are…(static)…CM, Longreach do

you copy?…Longreach CM five by five….CM are you reading the Lewis?…negative Longreach no contact, maybe they are having another wiring issue, solar flare or something?
CM can you see the Lewis…Negative! Longreach, I am 100 miles out! Can't see a thing, well, except the Moon… (Static noises) CM—Longreach, change to secure comms, over,…Roger Longreach.'

"This is a transcript of a radio conversation recorded in Australia (location secret). It reveals that something is wrong with the Lewis after it landed on the Moon. This was never released, and yet, has been assessed as an authentic recording. When the Lewis touched down on the 22nd of July 1967, this is what the rest of the world heard: 'Longreach, Grissom Base here, the Lewis made touchdown! Longreach: Great news Charlie we can all breathe again…Lewis: Sure thing Longreach we are go on all systems no warning lights over…Longreach: CM did you copy over…CM: You betta believe it, I followed the whole thing, nice job boys…Lewis: Thanks Aaron…don't you go wandering off now, we may need a lift home!… CM: I'll make sure of that Charlie, nowhere to go the bars are closed.'

Why did SEDA flood the airways with a radio conversation that gave voice to a perfect landing as part of a perfect mission, when Australia, had picked up a much juxtaposed signal? Truth is often stranger than fiction [Clue]. Of course I may have just published a hoax about a hoax, who knows. Strangely though, after reading through The Draper Diaries, I am not so sure. I use to be an ardent fan of the Athena achievements, now I am agnostic at best."

Well to say that the shit hit the fan would be a light handed description of the coming events. Southerby and the SEDA Director hounded Hugo. I was in his office at the time. The phone fight was seriously good television, if I had have had a camera. But the look on Hugo's face and the color of his skin had me concerned for my old friend. Our Twitter feed went viral, mainly with conspiracy theorists putting their own cases forward. There are more hoax theories and more subplots of hoax theories than I wanted to read. Like: Johnathon Livingston, a British publisher of New News Online, said photographs of the lander on the Lunar surface, would not prove that the United States put men on the Moon, and getting to the Moon really isn't much of a problem because both the Russians and the US have achieved that with many unmanned flights.

The big problem is not getting there, it's getting people there. He suggests that SEDA sent robot missions to the moon, due to high radiation levels in outer space being far too deadly for humans. Another variant on this is the idea that SEDA and its contractors did not recover quickly enough from the Athena 1 fire, and so all the early Athena missions were faked, with Athena Missions 14 or 15 being the first real missions.

Henry Ogilvie, a nuclear engineer, who self-published a book in 1982, Gravity is Everywhere, in which he disputes the Moon's surface gravity. Wayne Brighton, an American journalist and writer, produced a video called 'So you think we went to the moon'. In this video Brighton states that all of the Athena missions to the Moon were actually carefully rehearsed productions that were then filmed in large sound stages.

A retired American astronomy professor and conspiracy theorist, Dr. Abets defended his conspiracist views that all six Athena landings were hoaxes. Martin Albright who works for Open House Image Processing, examined the photo of Robertson emerging from the lander and said he can pinpoint when a spotlight was used. Using the focal length of the camera's lens and an actual boot, he allegedly calculated, that the spotlight is between 24 to 36 centimeters (9.4 to 14.2 in) to the right of the camera. This matches with the sunlit part of Drapers spacesuit. This goes on and on! Our twitter account made us look like the leader of false news. However, the leading world news agencies picked up the story and we were up and running internationally.

I was only back at the Ranch a few minutes when my phone rang. Cell phone call from Hugo: 'Virgil now the fucking website is down. What is going on?' Me; 'OK, OK I'll check it now Hugo, probably just a back-end problem.' Hugo; 'Shit! What if it's the NSA or FBI? Fuck that would put a spanner in the works!' Me; 'Can't find the issue.' Hugo; Why not for Christ Sake! I've got advertising to run.'

I couldn't find the issue because our back-end was down as well and I didn't want to add to his already high stress levels. I ran a ping and it timed out. I knew then that we were being hacked because we had an agreement with our ISP that the Domain must have redundancies to cover network failure. So they had mirrored the site in their domain server farm. One phone call and it was up again.

Even though this was the first time in ten years that our site was 'lost in space', all I could hear in my head was 'Danger! Danger! Mr. Smith'. Maybe Mr. Smith knew something. Whoever he was. With the help of the office crew, Hugo and I had the news feeds up and running in no time and the story re-published, with one addition.

'If our Government, or other forces, takes our ability away to Diaries the truth, we will find other ways to get The Draper Diaries out, because we are **Legion, we don't forgive and we don't forget, expect us.**'

It was a big gamble to add that to our website. Hugo wasn't sure that it was the right move. He considered it to be flippant, but he wasn't really in the mood to argue about it. I had doubts as well, but hey, I wanted to see if it opened or closed any doors for us. We were beginning to feel the heat and I knew the more we published from The Draper Diaries, the more heat would come our way.

I could see that we were going to face many problems with the government. No government likes to be accused of crimes and cover-ups and no government likes to be made a fool of. But it is our task as protectors of free speech that we continue with this action, and publish whatever the Anons had that showed misrepresentation to the people by the government.

Cell phone text from Cara: 'V, get out of the apartment now. SASS is coming to chat and I don't mean by the fireside.' Reply: 'Done!'

I grabbed my cell phone and laptop and headed to the Warren. Surely they wouldn't know about my hideaway. Apart from the spiders and their mighty constructions, I had a problem with mice. Every time I came down here I emptied traps and reset. It was dark and I only used low wattage LED lights. I never saw or heard the SASS goons arrive, but when I returned an hour later it was bloody obvious that the bastards had been there. Everything was trashed. Sofa cut up, bookcase smashed, bed destroyed, kitchen items all over the living room floor. WTF! Was that going to solve anything? If they thought The Draper Diaries were some big fat books, sitting out in the open in our apartment waiting to be hijacked, then God help the rest of the country, because these guys were stupid.

Cara was treading on thin ice now, if the Bureau caught wind that she had leaked operational information from any agency, she would be locked up. I was deeply concerned about how I was going to deal with the Diaries and keep Cara out of harm's way. Even though she was an experienced field agent, I always felt responsible for her safety. Cell phone text from Cara: 'V, I am being followed along Madison. I am going to Melanie's and try to lose them on the way. Call later. Stay Safe! Reply: 'All good here Babe, will meet you there.'

Melanie

Melanie was a friend of mine from our school days. A few years ago I intervened in the relationship she had with a violent coward, Peter bloody Dawson. Melanie had been suffering in silence until I saw her daughter on the tube. Gypsie was only 10 at the time and I remember thinking, that's too young to go wandering the tube alone. Gypsie told me that her mother was in serious trouble and that she had tried to end the relationship many times.

I had a brief close friendship with Melanie before I started at the Truth. I would visit her from time to time but it became difficult when the coward came on the scene. He was a church man, whatever that means, and he treated his partner like she was his own personal possession. She had to submit to everything he said. Even if it was wrong, immoral or just plain stupid. He would quote that ridiculous book, the bible, with words written up to five thousand bloody years ago, in times when women were less valued than a camel. People still, in these times of knowledge enlightenment, follow those fairy tales as if they were written in our own contemporary times.

But now gypsie was desperate as her mother's 'boyfriend' was becoming violent towards her also. I have always had zero tolerance for cowards. All women bashes are cowards. I went to see Melanie and physically threw her dirt bag out. I threaten him that if he came within cooee of Melanie and Gypsie, I had contacts that would take care of him. I didn't really, but it sounded real enough.

Following on from that I maintain contact with Melanie and Gypsie so I could monitor their safety, and keep them in contact with people who can give continuous support. Since then Melanie has been running a self-help group for victims of domestic violence with government funding. She has built a sense of place and has big plans for the future.

Gypsie is somewhat withdrawn and mostly hides away in darken rooms, or rides the tube for hours. She is extremely clever and has a very high IQ level. She is a bit of a computer nerd, but mainly plays online games. She doesn't attend school.

Melanie has an apartment on 5th avenue that the coward was renting from his church. Although I phoned her first to ask if it was not inconvenient, she as always, pushed that aside and lays out the welcome mat. She is a gem! At least at Melanie's, we would be able to chill out and maybe get Hugo around as well. Cara became friends with Melanie almost instantly on meeting her a year ago. They share a lot in common and both can be stubborn. I would have to get to Melanie's without the FBI knowing, because I am reasonably sure that she has never pinged a radar and it's best that it stays that way. Luckily the Warren had a hidden exit which led to a vacant lot that had been used as a community garden. Overgrown and littered with nasties, it gave me a good escape route. So back to the Warren and into the looking glass.

I took a Yellow to 5th Avenue. There were so many vehicles that I couldn't tell if I had been seen and followed. I was guessing that I had. The concierge let me in with a smile and a nod, he was used to me visiting, although I hadn't been there for a while. Melanie gave me a big hug as she always does. Cara wasn't there yet so I told Mel what was going down. Cara came a few minutes later she had done the old run around trick, and lost her tail in the corridors of the Metropolitan Museum of Art. That was too close for me as the Met is less than half a block away. Cara was getting concerned she believed the Anonymous group could be leading me into a trap, after all, I did write a scathing article about them a year ago. The article evoked an investigation into hacktivist and several key players were arrested both in the US and the UK.

Whilst I thought this maybe a point to consider, I wasn't showing any signs of alarm. I had a kind of sixth sense in regard to my articles. But Hey, that doesn't mean I am right. Cara tells me often that I am too trust worthy for my own good and that I should try harder to see the world from the other point of view. I know she is right and I do try. But it's hard to change character in the middle of a play.

We discussed the problems that were facing us. Once more Cara gave strong voice to letting the Anonymous issue slide. But she knew I wouldn't do that. Mel was being diplomatic and tried to ease the growing tension between Cara and myself.

I laid the points out. On July 16th 2017 anonymous hacks SEDA web-server. Website is down. On the 17th I wrote my first article on Athena and included a call to anonymous for more information. Mishin calls Hugo, pressure is on. Then I meet with Liberty Belle, and VPN to dark web. Released Cipriani's recording. Southerby gives

Hugo an ultimatum, cease and desist, or charges of treason may follow. LB invites me to Russian Consulate. Khovanski tells me the Yeltsin story. Publish another article, Hugo threatened once more and my apartment is trashed.

Not a lot to go on there, just a list of facts but no understanding what those facts will bring. All we knew was that Hugo was under the pump and I was being watched. Cara told us that she is definitely under surveillance and that means her job and career are in danger of imploding. Mel offered to help by running messages between Anonymous and myself. That was a good call because she is an unknown. I knew Mel messed about on the web and felt an allegiance to Anonymous, so this was going to be her way to fight back.

Our conclusion, with a noticeable frown from Cara, was to continue the publications and thereby force the hand of SEDA to call off the dogs and come to the table. Hugo wasn't called in for this meeting as we considered it too dangerous. He would have unwittingly lead the goons to the 5th Avenue apartment. Hugo was great at his job but had no sense of surveillance and couldn't pick a cop out of a crowd, let alone a spy. After-all, we may be monitored by SASS and they were not unlike the military Special Forces, but their Afghanistan was the streets of the USA. Cara decided to call her supervisor whom she trusted and try to get a handle on the situation.

Teddy Rollins was a 45 year old FBI careers man. Inducted before his honors degree was completed, he had missed several promotions. He believed that the powers-at-be saw him as old school and new blood was taking over, not just the FBI, but the whole world. Cara arranged to meet him in Central Park. Why is it that all the spies and FBI agents meet in Central? Maybe they have an affinity for the zoo animals (sorry Cara) after-all, they are locked up in protocol and secrecy for the rest of their lives, just as the animals are bound by cages. Hopefully Cara could push some tasty faux leads their way that will ease the pressure off her. Teddy informed Cara that she was under investigation for leaking information and that he had limited opportunity to help her. Teddy: 'Cara you shouldn't have recorded over the Russian tape. Some low level little nerd shit-head, recognized the over-recording from an earlier file.' Now they were convinced that Cara was a traitor. Teddy: 'I know you're not a crook Car, but once they have you in their sites, well you know what it's like.' Cara: 'Yeah like a dog with a bone.' Teddy: 'And Car— you know I am always looking out for you ah?'

Teddy was somewhat attached to Cara, although I know it was unrequited. He was going to fan some false flames towards the Russians to take the heat off Cara. If it didn't work Cara could find herself in a difficult situation. She will have to stay off the grid. Her reasoning was, that it is better to be wanted and not found, than to walk into a trap. So she decided to remain in the field, as it were, until things improve. It only gets worse.

My next article was due that afternoon. I planned to focus on the many dangerous problems that Charlie Draper found in the Lunar Landing Module, and how he complained bitterly about the 'bucket of bolts' that he and others are expected to put their trust in. Then leave a coded message to anonymous. In some ways it was unfortunate to have to release bits and bobs. However we were trying to keep the Truth out of serious trouble. Without the Truth, there would be no sponsors and no vehicle for Anonymous. So the story had to unfold with each upload. Public interest is hard to gain for any cause. Releasing the Diaries all at once would bombard the public with too much info and they would soon be over it. So like a well written song, we started slow and were building towards a crescendo that would linger for years.

The Truth News Online

July 21 2017

One Man's Junk

By Virgil Kaine

"Charlie Draper was a quiet, family orientated man, retired from the USAF National Hero after the Korean War. He was decorated several times and became an Ace war pilot. Working in Civvy Street as a flight and engineer instructor he soon became disillusioned with civilian life. A friend still serving in the USAF as a test pilot encouraged him to apply for one of the trainee astronaut positions with the newly formed SEDA. He did and was immediately accepted. His name would boost the validity of the space program and insure congress (all of whom loved war heroes) would continue to feed the umbilical cord.

Draper became disillusioned with the moon landings program after finding thousands of minor and many serious problems with the Athena lander. He once infamously described the spaceship as a 'bucket of bolts wrapped in tin foil'. He sent a detailed list of his findings on the Athena Lander to the chief engineer Rory Thompson. Thompson sent the letter onto the Managing Director. The list below is a fraction of what Draper found wrong with the Landing Module.

Problems with the LEM: Charlie Draper

I have been watching over the fit outs of the Athena Excursion Module at Longreach. This vehicle is not up-to-scratch as a space craft. There are so many problems I can't see how we are going to get it ready for the launch date. The hatch opens inward. Under pressure, if there is a need to escape, no astronaut will be able to open it. If there was a fire in space, astronauts would not be able to egress to relative safety. Which would mean we were doomed anyway as there is no plan B for a rescue from the Moon [clue].

I have shouted loud and often about this and always get the same reply. 'No problem Charlie we will look into it.' The place is crawling with mirror men. Below is a list of some main faults. I am extremely committed to beating the Russians, but if we do not come back alive, then one or many of these faults combined killed us.

Lunar Module Complaints

No protection against radiation. No fire escape plan from the pressurized Athena Excursion Module (LEM). The LEM often fails to re-compress after extra vehicular activities (EVAs) tests. Thousands of electrical faults have been noted. Flimsy construction (builders must be thinking that the landing will never happen, so they are using cheap materials and techniques in order to make a fortune). Rocket vibration may shake the LEM to pieces. To date it has not been tested. It is increasingly difficult to transmit by radio on the launch pad. So how are we going to communicate from another planetary body? Noise and vibrations are expected to be in the extreme. After all, we will be standing near the ascent module engine which sits directly above the descent engine.

Poor maneuverability inside LEM. Gas tanks are made from composite rubber and could easily be penetrated by rubble blown up from the moon's surface, as the outer skin of the LEM is ridiculously thin. Retro rockets were mounted too high and may tip the LEM over. There is no plan B if anything goes wrong. Even the shape worries the

other astronauts. It just doesn't look like a professional moon lander.
Charles Draper
November 1966.

Below is a memo found on a scanned document with the insignia of SEDA. It shows how Drapers complaints were swept under the carpet and the program pushed on with blatant disregard for the safety of the Athena astronauts.

Memo: RE: Charlie Draper

Astronaut Draper, in regards to the suitability of the LEM for a moon landing mission, has drawn my attention to the many problems he seems to have found. After considerable examination of the issues and after referring matters to the chief engineer, I have decided that time is of the essence. And that, the reassurance by the chief engineer has enabled me to give the Athena mission a GO status. Minor glitches can be resolved before launch time. It is my intention to informed astronaut Draper that his National Hero status should not be used to undermine SEDA, and that he should comply with his contract.

John Forbes Managing Director Athena Missions SEDA.

John Forbes has since past away. However, his decision placed the Athena crew in mortal danger, with no plan to extend the launch date until these matters were dealt with and the craft was deemed safe. I am asking the SEDA's current Director Rosealee Mishin, to come clean with the people of the USA and indeed the entire world. To-date, there has been no reply. Anonymous contact DP #1."

After this was published online, Mishin released a statement condemning the Truth News Agency and declaring me a cold blooded liar. She filed a law suit against the Truth and myself. Hugo wasn't concerned by such action. In his career many people and organizations had tried to muzzle free speech, but he always prevailed.

The District Herald

'The latest publication by the Truth News Agency belies their name, for the Truth is nothing more than the Lie. Virgil Kaine and Hugo Kent are trying to sell their own misdirection [clue] by joining up with the anonymous terrorist and faking the information published. SEDA has thousands of documents that support the Athena mission and its unfortunate ending. Why would we fake the deaths of three American Heroes?
Under extreme pressure from shareholders, to keep the Truth News Agency afloat, as a viable business, they have concocted these ridiculous claims in order to sell subscriptions to their online site. All I can say is SHAME

Virgil Kaine, you have placed a red mark across the name journalist, and destroyed the fundamental free speech and freedom of the press, rights, found in the 1st amendment of our great Constitution.'
Rosealee Mishin
Director SEDA

There are also charges pending for aiding and abetting of Anonymous (who have been declared a National security threat) by publishing secret messages: Anonymous contact DP #1. Hugo was not confident that we would get away with that. He wants me to arrange with Melanie to be the intermediary so the Truth can seem to be just Diariesing the facts and not actually involved in the plot. Of course, we already had.

Hugo

 Hugo Kent became a career journalist after working as a cadet in a mid-western country town's local rag. He has built his thirty three year career on his desire to achieve and his gut instinct in publishing stories. He will go to any lengths to expose a scam, investigate a politician, or give voice to the silenced. He is a tall man carrying more weight than he should and looking at times somewhat disheveled. Under the daily pressures of being the chief editor of a vital online broadsheet (as he preferred to call the Truth) he retreats often to his pal, Jack Daniels. Hugo and JD are inseparable. It wasn't uncommon for Hugo to pull old Jack out of his office desk draw and pour a shot or two: at any time of the day or night.

In the early hours of July 20 the Truth News Agency offices were broken into and all the computers were destroyed. Mild acid had been poured on the keyboards and the hard disk drives inside the computer cases had been smash with a hammer. When Hugo found the office in that state he immediately called me. Phone call from Hugo: 'Virgil, the bastards have smashed the office! The entire computer network is broken and everything is trashed. I'll have to rearrange the staff and get back online. Shit what a bloody mess.' Me: 'Leave it all for the NYPD Hugo and meet me at the Ranch. We can't let these bastards win.'

On his arrival, we setup a VPN and organized more mirror sites. Hugo knew about the Warren but he was far too large to move around down there with any comfort. So we stayed in the apartment. Each staff member would work from home and upload their relative articles. Things were escalating fast now but with Hugo's removable USB drive and my broken furniture holding us up, it was easy to get the next addition uploaded. As we were setting up some of the sponsors ads the site froze. Sponsors are the life blood of any news media site. We needed them as much as they needed us. At first, I thought it was the laptop but after rebooting the Truth was still down. That could only mean that SEDA had called in SASS, who was just as secret and untouchable as Anonymous, or the NSA was on the job.

We switched to an automatic mirror site replacement app, which Mel had obtained from Rev. I didn't know how she had achieved this at the time and I wasn't going to ask. Too many questions can make someone clam up, even if that someone is a friend. The App enabled our website to be kept continuously up even though IPs were being taken down. There was a tiny delay in the start of a new mirror which causes a momentary pause. We must have been driving those bastards crazy as we watched the number of flickers per minute. But hey, the Truth was online and would not be silenced! We finished our tasks with our golden motto raising a glass of JD. Hugo: 'The press is a free agent!' Me: 'And protected by the 1st amendment.' Tap of glass on glass.

Hugo wanted an immediate release of some more damaging evidence that would build greater support for The Draper Diaries column. The more support meant more pressure could be brought to bear from the Truths advertisers and shareholders onto the Government, to keep the news agency online in the public interest. This was a clever move by Hugo, because it not only gave him more punch in his corner, but also made money for the Truth. And let's face it, shareholders have to be kept happy or we are all out of work. Every one of us, everywhere.

The Truth News Online

July 22 2017

CapCom's Mardi Gras

By Virgil Kaine

"During the Athena Moon Landing mission in 1967 an astronaut called David Spitzer, held the position of CapCom. CapCom was short for capsule communicator and was the only person allowed to speak directly to the astronauts once they were in or beyond Earth orbit. There were logistical reasons for this but mainly so communications didn't become confused with a myriad of voices. Spitzer wrote in a personal diary, which was stored on the remote server at SEDA, that, he felt used by SEDA and he had failed the people of America by allowing himself to become a part of a treacherous event. Spitzer died in a car accident in 1968, when a goods train struck his 1967 Pontiac Fire bird [clue]. The authorities did not properly investigate the circumstances of the crash, as the funeral was bigger news. His body was burnt beyond recognition and only his SEDA astronauts' finger ring, was used to identify him [clue].

In his diary, he states that he was forced to fill in his communications to Athena with a scripted reply, if he received word in his earphones to do so. The occasion came about just before the LEM touched down on the surface of the moon. When he was receiving the order, a SASS agent placed his hand in front of the video camera being used in the command room at Longreach [clue]. Why? To block any view of Spitzer's fractured facial expressions as he was ordered to switch to his scripted replies, to a per-recording of events. Spitzer states that he was threaten and coerced to carry out SASS orders for the good of the Nation.

He knew that there was an alternative arrangement within SEDA to fake some parts of the moon landing if there was an embarrassing problem. He believed that some of the transmissions were faked, so SEDA could hide any minor problems from the world. However, later in 1968 he found evidence of the actual murderous plot. Over time he carried out a private investigation that SASS became aware of. He received a warning one night on the way home from SEDA Longreach. His car was stopped and two SASS agents told him in no uncertain terms, that he was to bury any thoughts of a conspiracy for the sake of his wife and daughters. 'Many accidents can befall a family' was the warning. He never told his family what happened as CapCom. It seems very strange that only a few weeks after the Moon landing, David Spitzer was killed in an automobile accident.

SEDA must respond immediately to this extremely serious accusation. Our readers and our sponsors are urging the space agency to come clean and deliver the truth. Only the truth will enable families to find closure, and only the truth will free future generations from this, our stained past. David Spitzer's family has been made aware of these allegations pre-publication."

Hugo left the Ranch and headed home. The next day we would need to clean the office and replace the equipment and hire security guards. That was going to take time and we didn't have the luxury of time on our side. I was getting worried about Cara. Normally I let a few days go by before I was concerned enough to break protocol and send her a text. But because she was now basically, on the run, I wanted to know where she was at all times.

Text to Cara: 'hey Babe, at the Ranch. Hugo has just left. Office trashed. Site OK with mirror. Contact pls.' After some time I received her reply. Text from Cara: 'V, see you at the Ranch in one hour. No more details on phones.' Cara returned to the Ranch with new information and lunch. How does she do it? She looked worn out and in need of a good sleep. Cara: I've been tracking Malina V. I think she is your mystery woman.' Me: 'Really? That actually makes some sense.' Cara: 'I want to interview her but I can't. So I think you should arrange an interview and try to dig out some facts. There are too many nibbles but very few bites. I have to get something on this Malina to give Teddy. If I don't those bastards are going to hang me out to dry: in public'. Me: 'Stay cool Cara, I will get her to talk. After-all babe, I am the smoothest talker in Manhattan.' Cara: 'Glad you think so V'. With a smile.

I didn't know how to contact LB so I logged onto the Deep Web chat site and hoped for the best. It wasn't long before I found her and arranged to meet at the Ranch for an interview on the Anonymous group. She agreed very easily. I was expecting some opposition as she has been so secretive. We were to meet the next day after dark. She would text me a coded message as she approaches our apartment: November 5 [clue].

The next morning I was expecting a call from Hugo about fixing the office. By lunch time I was getting concerned. Cara was out digging up clues and hopefully meeting with Teddy.

Phone call: NYPD: 'Mr. Kaine?' Me: 'yes'. NYPD: 'Mr. Kaine your editor Hugo Kent was found in 5th Avenue with serious injuries. It looks like he was mugged. His wallet is gone and a witness said two men took his brief case. Me: 'Jesus when was it, what hospital?' NYPD: 'Late last night. He is in the Lenox Hill Hospital. We have some leads but we need to speak with you ASAP.' Me: 'No problem I will go now to see Hugo and then I will be available.' NYPD: 'We would prefer if you spoke to the police before you see Mr. Kent.' Me: Shit mate, I've got to get to him. You can see me here at my apartment. Its number... ' NYPD: 'yes we know where you live. Stay put for now. Mr. Kent is in good hands and is sedated so he won't know you aren't there anyway'.

It only took three minutes for the door knock. They must have been in the area looking for me. Just before they called I was in the Warren, so there would have been no answer when they arrived the first time. I was pacing up and down the living room when the knock on the door came. It was clear to me after only a few questions that they had me in their sights. They needed someone to blame and they didn't care who as long as they had a result. Of course this was ridiculous. Hugo and I were old friends and had a sound working relationship. I could only guess that the FBI were the 'behind the scenes player' coaching the team from the side lines. I gave the abridged version of the Anonymous contacts and copies of the published articles. They seemed satisfied, at least for now. On to Hugo.

Hugo was a mess. His eyes were swollen and shut. His face was covered in graze marks and he had three broken ribs. No-one had interviewed him yet as the doctor had sedated him. The NYPD Diaries, as far as they could tell, or, wanted to release, showed that after leaving a local bar at

1:am, Hugo was seen by a CCTV camera being set-upon. There were a number of bystanders watching from across the street but they did not help him. One day they may need help and the same indifference will be their fate. However, it was a dark grainy film and gave little in clues. I needed to speak to Cara. Cara had a new cell phone and I didn't want to send her a TXT from my phone. There was only one option open to me, send an SMS from the Deep Web. SMS to Cara: DP #1. @1300. V.

I sat on the same seat where I was given The Draper Diaries. I was warm in the sun and Chinatown always looked colorful and exciting. It wasn't long before I saw my girl walking towards me. Cara had been busy. She was disguised as a punk with multi colored squares on the side of her head. That was unexpected. She had shaved her hair very short on the sides and left a floppy flap of hair on top. I barely recognized her. She looked, well, interesting. Me: 'Nice hair babe, love the colored squares.' Cara just smiled like she always does when complimented, kind of half thank you and half shyness. As we walked to Sheng Wang's for lunch, I got her up to speed with the newest events.
Me: 'Babe, Hugo is in Lenox Hill Hospital he was mugged last night or so the NYPD say. He may be there for at least a week' Cara: 'What! Shit, that's no mugging that's SASS passing a message to you both. This is going to blow any day now. We need a safe house.' Me: 'What about the Warren?' Cara: 'I knew you were going to say that. No fucking way, it's too dirty and it has creepies.' Me: 'Babe, the whole planet has creepies.' That didn't go down to well. But we still had to get our shit-in-order because we

couldn't keep putting Mel and Gypsie in danger. It just wasn't right. So we agreed the Warren was the safest place as very few people even knew it existed and it had multiple escape routes. It was close enough to 86 street station and Central Park and Lenox Hill, enabling us to get around and stay as much in the shadows as possible. Me: 'Did you see Teddy?' Cara: 'No, he is not answering his phone.'

Back at the Warren, I set up a crude cell phone aerial through one of the rusted down pipes. I had a mask ready to place over Cara's eyes or she just wouldn't be able to set foot in the Warren. We could get to the Ranch from an internal stairwell, so all was not lost as far as comfort goes. Keeping the blinds shut and drawing the curtains would make anyone know you are home. So we left the windows as they were. No lights. No TV. Appliances could be used downstairs, such as, microwave and electric jug. Homemade flat whites would replace cappuccinos. We slept in the Ranch (after we cleaned it up a little) and the Warren would be our Alamo. Now was the time to release more of the Diaries and see what type of rat crawls out from the sewer. I had to meet with LB at about 7PM.

The Truth News Online

July 23 2017

No Stars Perfect Shot

By Virgil Kaine

"The Draper Diaries stated that six people died during the Athena mission. Yet only three astronauts died in the infamous re-entry disaster. Why would someone add to the death toll and not publish it in 1967, along with the names and the reasons for their deaths? How can SEDA explain confusing radio signals from the moon in 1967? SEDA states it was UHF band bouncing of the Moon and the Earth. But this is NOT so. What did that Morse code signal recorded 50 years ago really mean? Can we really believe that the moon landings took place as we were told and history now teaches? There are so many questions that we have decided to release a full section of The Draper Diaries in this issue.

Athena Examination

Many people have examined the Athena moon photographs and concluded that these are fake. Stage sets of a Lunar landscape and false craters on the planet Earth's ground that look exactly like moon craters, have been Diariesed in Area '51, a closely guarded military base in Nevada. Even at Longreach there is a Lunar dome that exactly represents the surface of the Moon. One of the many complaints about the Athena photographs is the lack of stars.

No stars, even though the moon has a low albedo especially from standing on its surface. Albedo is the reflective index of a surface. As an example, the albedo of worn asphalt is 0.12 and the reflectivity of snow is 0.80 to 0.90. The albedo of the moon is 0.13. The Earth on the other hand has an albedo of 0.38. So the moon is only fractionally more reflective than worn asphalt: common old road surface material. That means, the reflection of the sunlight off the Moon's surface would not impinge on the ability of an astronaut, or his camera, from seeing stars in the pitch blackness of outer space. The brightness of the Moon as seen from Earth appears to be high. This is because we are seeing, at full moon, more than half the Moon's surface area. Divide the number of square meters of Lunar surface by 0.13 and you can see why the astronauts were only seeing a tiny fraction of the reflected light off the Lunar surface.

Not all the light reflected is aimed at an astronaut's body. Reflected light generally goes straight back into outer space. Outer Space is a vacuum and a vacuum has no elements, such as an atmosphere that can reflect light. When standing on the Moon, the astronauts would be in outer space. There is no atmosphere to divide the Moon's surface from the emptiness of space. Therefore, the reflected light is not defused, it travels in a straight line towards the Earth or beyond. Even when facing away from the Sun the Athena photographs show no stars. Sunlight cannot diffused and illuminate space. Nothing can illuminate the blackness of space. The astronauts would have encountered a pitch black 'Lunar sky' with millions of stars.

The Sun in many of the images is far too large. It has been said that this is because of camera lens flare. But lens flare is an atmospheric condition. Again we return to the fact that there is no atmosphere around the Moon that can enlarge the Sun's image via atmospheric magnification. Furthermore the Sun in reality, is the same size from the moon as it is from earth. Although the Moon is 250,000 miles closer to the Sun than the Earth, that distance is minuscule when compared to the actual distance the Earth is from the Sun: 94 Million Miles. If the Sun were as large as we see in the Lunar photos, then it would be impossible to see a Lunar eclipse from Earth.

The still photos from the Moon mission were stunning: a very professional job. The astronauts took thousands of pictures, each one perfectly exposed and sharply focused. Not one of them was badly composed or even blurred. Some say that the astronauts had long practice periods to learn how to use the cameras. However when looking at the clumsiness of astronauts trying to use the cameras on the 'Moon's surface' it suggest that no matter how much training they had, it would be impossible to frame and focus every picture perfectly. I use a modern digital camera set on automatic and I still can produce bad photography.

The TV broadcast was almost impossible to watch and many of the scenes in the film were not the same as in the photographs. Why? Were they all faked here on Earth? Even their film stock was unaffected by the intense cosmic radiation on the Moon. These conditions should have made any film useless [Kaysing].

The astronauts managed to adjust their cameras, change film and swap filters in pressurised gloves. It should have been almost impossible to bend their fingers. So how did they achieve something that only a free hand can do?

It has been said that the Moon landings could not have been faked because it is obvious that the astronauts are in 1/6th Earth gravity and after-all, a hammer and feather experiment was conducted where both a solid hammer weighing, on Earth, about four pounds, and a birds feather weighting only 0.03 of an ounce, were dropped at the same time and hit the Moon's surface at the same time. However, all one needs to complete that experiment is a large vacuum chamber. Why? Because it is the Earth's atmosphere that stops the feather from falling at the same speed as the hammer. Therefore there must be a vacuum chamber on Earth large enough to house a Lunar landing Module. And guess what? There is such a chamber. The Herschel Research vacuum chamber, in Verona, is 100 feet in diameter and 122 feet tall. The LEM (Lunar Exploration Module) is only 22 feet in height and 31 feet wide. This gives a lot of space for SEDA to build a moon set within a vacuum.

The shadows in the Moon photos show multiple angles. Only extra lighting could have created these shadow discrepancies, and no extra lighting source was taken to the moon as lighting requires a lot of electricity. The only real light source when on the Moon is the Sun. So where did all these intersecting shadows come from? The Myth Busters program built a tiny unrealistic Lunar Scape and used a light source without mathematically determining light values in comparison to the Sun, and said that they had busted the Moon Hoax myth. Yet they had the multiple light sources required to produce a perfect television grade video. They actually manipulated the fake lunar surface to produce their required outcome.

Even the American flag waved in a breeze when there is no atmosphere to cause a breeze. SEDA states that the flag moved because Charlie Draper was twisting the flag pole. But it seems to move much more than it should even when Draper is not twisting the flag pole.

A SEDA public affairs officer Adrian Bellows, once delighted several hundred guests at a private party, with footage of astronauts apparently on a Lunar landscape. It had been shot on a mission film set and was identical to what SEDA claimed was the real Lunar landscape. He boasted that he was a part of the filming and that everything was fake.

The Lander weighed 2.83 tons (in 1/6 gravity) yet the astronauts seem to have made a bigger dent in the dust with their boot prints than the lander made with its landing pads. SEDA says that the silica content of the regolith when compressed (magically) clings together to form a positive mould of the underside of the astronauts boots. So why hasn't anyone been able to reproduced that effect in a vacuum chamber?

The powerful booster rocket (throttled down to 2000lbs just before touchdown) at the base of the Athena Lander, left no traces of blasting on the regolith (soil) underneath. It should have created a small crater, yet the booster looks like it's never been fired.

Even when the ascent module takes off from the Moon to return to orbit and dock with the Santa Maria, no rocket exhaust is seen. The ascent engine sat on top of the descent module therefore, the landing stage of the LEM would have been all but destroyed by the power of the ascent modules rocket engine. Yet we now see images of the Moon Landing sites showing (supposedly) the landing module's still intact on the Moon's surface, When they should be a crumbled mess.

Why didn't SEDA alert the Athena Command Module crew that a rogue satellite was on a collision course with them? Why didn't the crew make adjustments? They could have complete another orbit to escape the satellite and then do a re-entry burn. Nothing was tried to save them. Even though we are expected to believed implicitly that the events took place, we must now ask more questions, about Athena and the astronauts deaths."

That article caused an avalanche of emails. The Truth server momentarily froze as people from all over the world condemned us for trying to rewrite history. What a crock of shit. Do these sheep really think that our governments are always truthful and are out to do the best for us at all times. Governments are there for themselves. They have strayed away from their intended purpose of securing a safe community. They do the exact opposite. They build a false impenetrable wall around their systems and govern, as if, they have a God given right. Any-one who thinks otherwise is living in a dream world.

Malina

At the time, no-one knew who Malina was and certainly no-one knew her last name: Georgiou. The FBI had discovered evidence of a foreign spy entering the US via the old Rio Grande. She has been sent by a secret group of Russian's associated with the Kremlin. They want to revive the old Soviet Union and return Russia to (as they see it) its former glory. Malina has been trained in explosive, surveillance and assassinations.

At 7Pm Text Msg from LB: November 5. Me: 'All clear.'

She came in and hurried me to close the door. This was a woman who watched her own back. Cara was down the road with Teddy in a van. The Ranch was bugged and they were recording. Me: 'Well LB, drink?' LB: 'What? What is LB Mr Virgil?' Me: 'Oh that's just a name I gave you because you wouldn't tell me your name. I can't keep calling you. hey you. So I call you Liberty Belle.' LB: 'That's a strange name, why liberty belle?' Me: 'Well, liberty because we were talking about it at the time and Belle because, well, you are a good looker. If you don't mind me saying so?' She laughed it off leaving me to wonder if I had complimented her, insulted her, or, if she thought I was some sort of sleaze. Hopefully not the latter.

Me: 'What should I call you?' LB: 'Belle is nice, let's try that.' Me: 'Okay. When you contacted me did you have information that could help Anonymous or were you on a fishing trip.' Belle: 'I don't like fishing Mr Virgil. I wanted to help Anon: Revenge, to expose government corruption.' Me: 'But you are with the Russian Consulate aren't you?' Belle: 'No not really. I am friends with Vasily. I have known him for years. I am not Russian.' Me: 'Yeah I gathered that. Your Greek accent still comes through your Russian overlay.' Belle: 'Of-course.'
 We kept the chat up for an hour. She told me that she was linked to Anonymous and wanted the Truth to expose any

secrets of the Government that the people should know about. So why America? Why not Russia? So I questioned her more about the Yeltsin story told to me by Khovanski. She said he believed that it was recorded in The Draper Diaries by Charlie Draper himself, and that the US had used it as leverage on many occasion. Apparently, what Khovanski wanted was for me to lose the recording transcript. Sorry Mr Vasily, but it's too important to hide any longer. I believe it may be linked somehow, to the Athena disaster [Clue].

I wasn't so sure that Belle was with Anonymous. She seemed too cultured and people like her didn't fit the profile of a restless civilisation misanthrope. At the end of our little chat, I really wasn't sure what I was doing or who I was talking to. This woman knew how to lead a journo around her metaphysical maze by the proverbial nose ring. When LB now Belle, left, Cara and Teddy came in. Teddy showed me some photos of me and Belle in Battery Park. I was a little confused until Cara told me that this Belle, had been under surveillance for some time. The FBI and NSA did not want to arrest her before they worked out what she was here for. Sound enough reasoning I suppose. But that left me as a contact for her and therefore a person of interest to them. Then Cara said that Belle is probably Malina and that she is up to no good. Now we both needed to find out what was going on.

I told Teddy about the Yeltsin recording and that I intended to publish it to rattle a few cages. He said it may be a mistake and back-fire, but, that it wasn't his job to run other people's lives. I guess that's why he was passed over for promotion. He was a decent guy.

May 26th 1961

"Our transmission begins now...Forty one...this way...forty one...Yes...I feel hot...I feel hot... It's all...It's hot...I can see a flame! What? I can see flames! I can see flames! I feel hot...I feel very hot...Thirty two...My children...My children...Save them...Am I going to crash?

Yes...yes... I feel hot! I feel very hot! I will re-enter! I will re-enter too fast, too steep...wrong way around...I am listening! I feel hot! I am burning please help what can you do? Spinning madly...get me home please...I am burning...static and screaming...

You have just read a transcript of a horror story. A horror story told from outer space. In May 26th 1961 a CIA operative, recorded a radio conversation between what he believed was the Soviet Union's space agency and a female cosmonaut. The first human in space. The woman was in serious trouble as her primitive space capsule was spinning uncontrollably and losing altitude. If this continued, she would re-enter the Earth's atmosphere the wrong way around and be burnt alive.

What must she have been thinking as the capsule began to heat up well beyond safe levels? She saw flames as the space craft began to burn. Spinning so fast her vision would start to blur and her blood would be centrifuged to her body's outer extremities. She was plummeting to Earth

7
1

at over 20,000 kilometres per hour. She had no chance. And as if to rub salt into her wounds, a voice can be heard saying, 'STOP SCREAMING YOU ARE SOVIET COMMUNIST. DIE LIKE MAN Bitch!' To this day the Russian's have failed to acknowledge the recording with any reply. Did this happen to Charlie Draper, Ed Robinson and Aaron Rosenbach as well, or did they die from an entirely different fate? [Clue]

All the worlds' media was covering the latest release of The Draper Diaries. Questions were put to historians and journalist alike. Most of it was the usual rubbish that is spouted when a government faces charges by the media. The Russian Embassy in Washington DC made a direct rebuttal to the media. They stated that the entire thing was a cruel hoax, perpetrated by the enemies of Russia and that it should not be considered as a true fact."

Live CCCPN news

The Russian Government is deeply hurt by the latest release of the so called Diaries on the so called Truth News Website. The Truth is obviously running false news as this seems to be a part of American news media culture. Our cosmonauts were all treated with the utmost respect throughout the Space Race and since. All our missions are on public record and nothing in the Truth is real.

The former Soviet Union was a peaceful nation conducting a social experiment in order to save the world from greed. It would never have placed the lives of our brave and heroic cosmonauts in danger.

The Russian Government demands a complete retraction of the published lies and will require the USA Government to openly apologise to the Russian people. We will not lie down and watch our reputation tainted by false news zombies at the Truth. The Kremlin has ordered all non-accentual embassy staff home and will be reviewing the very existence of the American Embassy in Moscow.

Not since 1967, when Russia was blamed for the incompetency of SEDA, have we been so insulted. The USA would do well to hunt down this traitor of peace Virgil Kaine and lock him away in Guantanamo for the safety of its citizenry.

Vasily Khovanski

Special Minister"

Well that put the cat amongst the pigeons, and let me know what Khovanski's job was: shit stirrer. Washington tried to play down the whole thing saying that the Truth had gone too far, but in the US freedom of speech was a God given right. Of course behind the scenes the NSA and FBI were chomping at the bit, to cut me down. I hoped that what I had done would not be in vain. It was a gamble to pin the Russians down on the canvas of media rumour.

However, in order to cut them free, so that I could release more of the Diaries without causing embarrassment to the Russians, or create an international incident, I decided to remove the one thing that Khovanski said he was worried about. If the US couldn't dredge up old secrets because I had already exposed them, then all should go well. Sometimes my naivety shocks me.

Late that night the Truth News office was torched. But by whom, US forces or Russian spies? The NYFD managed to keep the fire local and that in its self was a bonus. But for us, that meant no more interactive work space. We would all have to work from home.

Cell Phone from Hugo: 'Virgil I heard about the Truth offices on the news. This is serious now. First I am set upon now we are burnt out. I am convince that the content of that Diaries will be the biggest story since Christ walked on water.' He was right. Something had the parties concerned, shrinking in fear and causing them to act irrationally with no empathy for others. This was becoming a dangerous situation.

Cara and I were trying to relax and have a home cooked meal at the broken Ranch, when someone tried to kick the door in. **Bang! Bang!** Then voices and finally splinters of wood as the door shattered and three burly men rushed in all wearing black mask. I had left Cara's FBI issued glock in the damn Warren after cleaning it as a favour for her. Stuffed up there ah! As I was struggling with the assailants I screamed at Cara to go to the Warren. **Alamo! Alamo!** At least there she could be armed and able protect herself. I saw her run to the bathroom, she was chased by one of the goons. I put up a strong fight but I was overcome with something from a plastic bottle.

When I regained consciousness, I guessed I was in a large open building by the echoes of voices and the drafty atmosphere. Something like a cold, dark damp warehouse. I was tied to a chair. Very original. As soon as I showed signs of being conscious the chair was laid back and water was tipped over the cloth bag they had placed on my head. Let me tell you all now, water boarding is a complete arse. It is so hard to breathe and every breath is a struggle to not inhale water. They wanted me to sign a confession stating that the Russian cosmonaut transcript was false. A hoax put together by the CIA to further embarrass the Russian President who recently had condemned accusations, that he was involved in the cyber espionage during the US presidential election campaign. I refused! More water.

After several more attempts at drowning me (which I don't mind saying that if they had persisted more I may have cracked) I heard a woman screaming. In the confusion of the event I must have associated the screams with Cara. I called her name. Voices laughed. More screams. More laughter. I struggled to get free and ended up on the floor still tied to the chair. Me: 'You mother fuckers, I will kill all of you for this. Let her go!' Reply voice: 'Laughing, Mr Virgil, the longer you take to sign, the more your Cara will suffer. And when the boys are finished they will rape and kill that spying bitch!' Then more screams. It sounded like my girl. My mind was spinning. What could I do to save her? I was spent. It was then I knew I had to do a David Hicks and sign, anything to try and save her and worry about the consequences later. Of course that could mean that we were both dead after that. So should I sign? Ah that's me all over, always trying to out think myself.

As they pulled the hood off my head... Cara: 'FBI! Don't fucking move!' Shit my girl was standing behind the goons, arms out stretched, holding her beautiful Glock. I love that Glock. She must have looked very strange to the goons. Multi coloured squares in her hair, slim build with a demon look. Cara: 'Hands on heads and knees on the floor scum.' She had a way with words. I think only a couple of them had guns and they were holstered at the time, which gave them no chance to challenge Cara. Cara: 'Lose the guns. Now!' Two of them tossed their weapon across the floor. Cara: 'Any move to those weapons and your fucking dead!' I loved it when she talked tough.

She was cutting the cable ties, when one of the goons tried to get something from under his coat. As I was about to warn Cara, she caught my expression and only had to do a quarter turn to fire one round into his shoulder. They all froze. The wounded guy was in real pain trying to grab his shoulder. But each time he tried Cara would shout 'hands up!' At last I was standing free. Well, free of the chair at any rate.

The FBI agent, with the pretty hair, motioned me back with her left hand on my chest. Her right arm still out stretched holding monsieur Glock firm and straight at them. We walked backwards to a side door. Goon: 'You cannot win Mr Virgil! You and your bitch dog are doomed!'

As we turned and ran out to the open yard between several warehouses, Cara tossed a smoke grenade back through the door. I wasn't expecting that! That would give us a split second or two to get a head start. They followed. Shots rang out from behind. I caught one in the left leg, just above the knee. 'Fuck!' It tore through the surface flesh. Cara returned fire like the well trained operative she was. Later we discovered that she had wounded two of them, but they never showed up at any hospitals according to Teddy. Dashing up an alley way, half dragged by my little hero, we reached her stolen car. Two rounds pierced the back windscreen and cracked the front windscreen. I had a wounded leg, but hey, I love fast cars. We were out of there like a formula one pole position driver on the green light.

Me: 'Great shooting babe!' Cara: 'When!' Me: 'Getting that goon in the shoulder.' Cara: 'Are you fucking mad V? I was aiming for his head.' A goon's van followed us. But they had no hope catching me in New York. All I had to do was get out of Brooklyn and head for Harlem, plenty of places to hide there.

We drove wildly through the streets followed by some crazy Russian bastards. Cara: 'They're not from the Russian Consulate.' Me: 'Unless they hired some muscle?' They were gaining on us. Cara was going to put a round into the hood of their van to try and kill the engine. Dangerous and tricky in the open streets of NYC with plenty of night time traffic. But lo and behold she did hit the van, not in the hood, but in one of the front tyres. The van swerved and crashed into a maintenance barrier. Me: 'Hey now that was great shooting babe!' Cara: 'Oh yeah right.' There were sirens wailing and I could see the flashing lights way up ahead. So a quick turn into an alleyway and we ditched the car. It was shank's pony now and sticking to the shadows.

Later Cara told me about her escape at the broken Ranch, she had broken away from one man's grip by kicking him in the family jewels and ran into the bathroom locking the door behind her. That gave her enough time to shimmy down the outside sewer pipe and into the warren, via the looking glass. She had used her cell phone as a torch and had to crawl on hands and knees to avoid the spider webs and any arachnids. How she did that is a mystery to me. It just goes to show what can be achieved when your life or a loved one's life is in danger. Finding her Glock she raced outside in time to see me being man-handled into a white van. She car jacked a Mercedes-AMG GT and used the tracker that she had sown into my jacket: clever girl. Then it was just the case of finding a way in to the building where I was being held without being seen, so she could get the drop on the goons. And boy did she drop them!

Brown Bread

I was now convinced that SASS and the Russians were in league together. Something big needs to be done to blow the dust away and get a clear view of the players involved. There was plenty in The Draper Diaries that could be released. The problem was, what?

The breaking news the next day was that the Russian Consulate computer system had been hacked and hit with a denial of service. Anonymous could get thousands of people on the Deep Web to hit any server system all at once. They left a message on the screens of each PC connected to the Web. 'Revenge for V! Your files are encrypted. To unencrypt these files you must release a media statement saying that Russia has been meddling in US politics and is sorry for torturing an American citizen. If they admitted to that, the US would have no option but to close the Consulate and cut off all ties with Russia. Would the US President have wanted that to happen? I was trying to work out how Anonymous knew about me being snatch from the Ranch. We hadn't told Melanie yet, or Hugo [clue].

There was no media release from the Russians. Instead, they had enacted their contingency plans and restored their computer systems. I have to take my hat off to them, if indeed I wore one of those things. They must have had everything backed up to the finest detail and to the very second before Anonymous hit them. So many individuals and companies, failed to run apps to correctly backup their systems and store those backups off site and off the Net. But at least Anonymous showed they are still a force to be reckoned with and that Anon: Revenge was calling the shots. Even if unofficially.

My next step, after receiving treatment for my wounded leg by a dodgy after hours doctor, was to write a Column with as big a blow to the Russkies as I could dig out of the Draper Diaries. Maybe we will go too far? Maybe someone will get physically hurt (more than I have been) or maybe someone will die? Maybe we will win? And, maybe we will lose? Who knows these things?

The Truth News Online

July 27 2017

Misdirection

By Virgil Kaine

"Our friends at Anonymous have recently uncovered more secret files held on antiquated UNIX servers in long forgotten university basements. It is well known that a great deal of research for the Space Race was conducted at specialist universities. A document has been discovered that supports previous hoax allegations that Yuri Gagarin was not the first human in space, although he may have been the first man in space: or not. The document was written in 1963 by an unknown source. It states that the CIA knew that Gagarin's flight was a fake. However, The US and the Soviets had already made an unofficial pact to build and maintain a Space Race, in order to give both economies a much needed boost.

In 1961, the world believed that a Soviet Air Force officer, Yuri Gagarin, became the first person to travel in space. However, a Soviet cosmonaut, Vladimir Ilyushin, was rocketed into space on 7th of April, 1961: 5 days before the announcement of Gagarin's flight. The US intercepted several radio communications between Ilyushin and the Soviets. Ilyushin's soft landing failed and he was seriously injured. To cover-up this failure, the Soviet Union's propaganda machine, claimed that his injuries were as a result of a car accident and that he was sent to China to receive advanced medical treatment.

The Russian TV documentary Cosmonaut Cover-Up (2001) also claims that on 7th of April, 1961, Vladimir Ilyushin left for space, got into trouble during the first orbit, and crash-landed in China during the third orbit. Ilyushin was badly injured. He returned to the Soviet Union a year later. Ilyushin died ironically, in a real car accident later that year.

Radio Moscow claimed that a Soviet cosmonaut, Yuri Gagarin, traveled into space on the morning of the 12th April, 1961, with the space-rocket Mostok. According to the official announcement, he had already landed and was in fine health. The whole world believed this except for the Western intelligence services. They had not managed to register any radio communication between Gagarin and the Soviet space center.

In a Diaries written for the West, Soviet propagandists claimed that, 'simple' peasants recognized Yuri Gagarin soon after he had parachuted onto a field near his old parachute training school, some 200 kilometers off course. And enthusiastically shouted: "Gagarin, Gagarin!" At the time, nothing about his 'space journey' was Diariesed. The reaction of the farmers was strange, given that he was an unknown until his propaganda marketing. No pictures of him had ever been published and his name had not been mentioned.

The newspaper Sovetskaya Rossiya, claimed that Gagarin was wearing a blue flight suit when he landed. In his memoirs, Gagarin himself claimed he was dressed in an orange flight suit. At his press conference, Gagarin read from notes when he spoke of his journey. Gagarin made several mistakes when discussing his space flight. He said that he could see the whole Earth, yet never discussed what he saw. Photographs of him sitting in his spacecraft, supposedly in orbit, were actually taken in a training capsule bolted to a floor here on Earth.

Foreign journalists wondered when the photographs that Gagarin supposedly took in space would be published. When asked this question, at first Gagarin was silent. He thought for a moment and then said, 'I didn't have a camera with me!' Sending a man into Low Earth Orbit before the USA, was the most important propaganda coup for the post WWII Soviets. Therefore, to publish Gagarin's pictures from space would have been a vital priority! The Soviet Union would never have missed an opportunity like that. In contrast, Allan Shepard, the first American into space, had his photographs cabled out immediately.

When Gagarin was disillusioned with the charade and let it known that he wanted to actually orbit the Earth, he was 'killed' in a plane crash. After being forbidden for years from flying, all of a sudden permission was granted. His plane exploded on March 27th, 1968. The official Diaries concerning this event contained many contradictions. The Diaries was classified during the communist period. It claimed that Gagarin's body could not be found. That being the case, how did his flight jacket end up buried deep in the mud inside the crashed jet trainer, yet no body attached? [clue] Was it normal practiced for jet fighter pilots to remove their jacket once in the cockpit? I think not.

Now we can reveal that Anon: Revenge, has found information that tells a different story. A story of how Gagarin was chosen to represent the Soviet cause **as a mascot**, and not as a true cosmonaut. An interview in 1980 with a protected Russian x-spy has shed light on the Gagarin truth.

Translation: 'I overheard Alexei Yenin (Chief Personal Manager) tell Vlad Babanin (Assistant State Strategist), that 'Yuri Gagarin will not fly in space. He is of great importance to the Soviet cause. My order on this matter is to fake it and give USA a kick in the arse. Under no circumstance will USSR permit Yuri Gagarin, cosmonaut state hero, to risk his life in space. Not even for Nikita Sergeyevich Khrushchev.'

The Soviets were playing a game not against the USA, but, with them. More revealing evidence that will be published at a later date, will shock you all, with its damning proof of a US-Soviet combined cover-up."

Cell phone 0300 from Hugo: 'V they're trying to kill me! [Heavy breathing] [Gunshot, Something falling] Press is always…'[Some traffic noises] Me: 'Shit! Hugo, what's happening? Are you in trouble? Where are you?' Hugo: 'go on then brother [clue], shoot.' [Gunshot x2] No problem old man. Me: Hugo! Hugo!...Hugo [Russian accent]: 'Shut the fuck up with all the leaks and other shit or you will die all.' The call dropped out. Cara was awake now. I explained that it sounded like Hugo had been shot and that someone with a Russian accent had spoken into Hugo's phone. Why did he say 'Go on brother…'[clue] was that a code? They were obviously Russian but maybe not regular spies.

We left in a Yellow to Hugo's apartment, but he wasn't there, next, a text to Mel. She hadn't seen him. Then Mel said that Gypsie had monitored NYPD cell phone traffic and thinks there is something big going down at the back of the Guggenheim [clue]. My first thought was, how could a 15 year old school kid monitor NYPD cell phone traffic? And, why would she want to?

Cara and I headed to the Guggenheim, discreetly. This was no time to be arrested, mugged or kidnapped: again. My leg was a concern I could feel the warm blood under the bandages. That would be very hard to explain at the scene of a shooting. We kept low in the park opposite E 87th Street. There were several 'Smart fortwo [sic] Hatchbacks' parked outside the Guggenheim and an Interceptor utility, all flashing red and blue lights. I wanted to get a closer look but it was risky. Cara said she knows who it is. She told me to hold where I was and she would question one of the onlookers. She strode over to the back of a small crowd that had gathered on the opposite side of the street corner. I could see her talking with someone. Then she took a long look and headed back, sticking to the shadows.

Cara: 'V, its Hugo, sorry.' Me: 'Fuck!' I stood up angrily shaking. That was sickening news. She had to pull me back down into the bushes. If we were seen, I had no chance to out run them. And we had far too much to explain to the local cops to get ourselves caught. Like why were we there? And, why were we hiding in the bushes? Part of me answered my own question with a question. Yes why were we hiding? Shouldn't I just go over there and talk to them, or at least see Hugo for myself? But I knew the best course of action was to follow Cara's lead, after-all, she was the trained field agent not I. Me: 'and protected by the 1st Amendment.' Cara: 'What?'

The Warren

There were no ifs about it now. The Warren was home base. The game had just turned deadly. I promised Cara I would sweep out all the spider webs as we crawled through the back entrance to the Warren. Quickly I set about making the janitor's room clean enough to keep Cara's anxiety attacks at bay. I had hammocks in a tin trunk that I could string across the room. She insisted on plenty of bug spray being kept there. So I liberally poisoned all my Warren mates: *Lest we forget*. Food and other human necessities would be a challenge, but for now we had to get some rest.

We knew that the apartment building was now under continued surveillance. Luckily we had a secret entrance. The old community garden was about the size of two suburban front yards: depending where you lived. It was totally over grown and was once frequented by drug users. The NYPD sorted that out and now it lies quietly in ruin. Behind an old water tank is a long forgotten wooden door that we could just squeeze in and out of. Staying low we could track the shadows of the trees and weeds to easily get onto the street unseen. I knew it wouldn't be long before someone saw one or both of us. Previously I had only used the 'emergency' exit as a bit of fun. Little did I know that I was training for the real thing.

As long as we cooked in the janitor's room no light would be seen. Once I had the place in order I told Cara to remove the hood I placed over her head. No seriously, if she had have watched me clean away spider webs and tread on spiders, she would have been out of there, like a bullet from her glock.

I connected my makeshift cell phone aerial and surfed to WABCTV. There was a tiny breaking news line. Unidentified man shot and killed near the Guggenheim, Police on scene, more to follow. It was not safe to use our cell phones direct to each other, but we could SMS from the deep web and that is how were planned to stay in contact.

The Truth News Online

July 30 2017

Death Notice

"It is with a heavy heart that the Truth must announce the death of our Editor and friend, Hugo Kent. Hugo was shot and killed outside the Guggenheim in the early hours of July 30 2017.

Hugo was a giant in his field and never compromised to weaken a story. Lately he had been harassed by government agencies and a foreign power to stop publishing The Draper Diaries. Hugo had great insistence on morality and professional ethics. He was cut down by assassins, that, we are sure of. Who hired them, we do not know: yet.

There is a memorial being held at the Lower Manhattan Community Church, at 9 AM Monday.

RIP Hugo Kent."

We certainly underestimated the number of people who attended the memorial service. Melanie sent a message about the numbers of people. Some of them wore Anonymous masks. It was a small non-denominational church, with an outreach ethos. Hugo liked it and often visited. Of course Cara and I could not attend. That would only lead to talk and suspicion. But we had no alternative, by now we were suspects in Hugo's murder, after-all, I had been a suspect in his bashing. The cards were being stacked against us so we had no-where to run. It wouldn't be long before the Warren was discovered, and then what? Time for some pay back: Journo style.

The Truth News Online

August 01 2017

Moon Shot

By Virgil Kaine

"The Draper Diaries is continuing to divulge many hidden truths. By the time this series is complete the world will be made fully aware of the callous and murderous plots of the Space Race. Plots, which were enacted by both antagonists. Below are a series of document releases that outline a secret relationship between the USA and the Soviet Union. It was a marriage of convenience, for both sides knew that no-one could win a nuclear war. The cost of such an attack would be world annihilation.

MOU: Sasha Ivakin. Soviet Space Agency. 1966.

To: Chief Assistant Director KGB

It is with concern, comrade that I write to you in regard to our manned mission to the moon. Data from Lunar probes have dealt the Soviet Union a crushing blow. Much that we hoped for cannot be achieved without the loss of cosmonauts. These losses would be used by USA to condemn our great revolution and all the achievements that it has produced.

We know there is no atmosphere around the moon. We also know that trying to reach Lunar orbit has been fraught with troubles and disasters. Over shots are common and I cannot blame our glorious space program leaders, however, it does seem to be a game of folly. Radiation levels on the Moon's surface are at the extreme. The Radiation area that shrouds the Earth from ~1,000 kilometers out, is so severe that we have lost dogs on several occasions. Now we have to contend with the fact that our latest mission has failed.

As you are aware, we launch three days ago. The spacecraft was to take two of our best and most loyal cosmonauts to orbit the Moon before making a soft landing. After which, they would re-enter their Lunar orbit and make the journey home. We would have beaten USA and triumphed. The Soviet cause would have been highlighted and many countries would seek our assistance. But alas that is not to be.

Our brave cosmonauts, a man and a woman, have perished while traveling through the radiation belts that shroud our planet. Their space craft has over shot the Moon and is headed for a heliocentric orbit around the Sun. It is our considered opinion that landing a manned spacecraft on the surface of the Moon at this stage, in our technological

development, is impossible. Of Course this has been classified Top Secret and is for your eyes only.
Sasha Ivakin

Communique 1966

Director KGB Space Operations

Director KGB Foreign Operations

Sasha Ivakin, Soviet Space Agency, has informed me that the moon missions are impossible without the loss of cosmonauts. I enclose a folder of scientific evidence that you may want to show USA. After-all if they kill their astronauts on moon missions, it will look very bad for the Soviet Union, if anyone finds out that we knew, manned moon missions were not possible.

Научные (Scientific) отчет (Diaries)
Translation: Manned Moon mission developments.
Radiation levels in the Van Allen Radiation Belt region are extremely high. Diariesed between 0 and 100 rad [clue]. Beyond this belt open space has even higher radiation and it is known that Lunar probes have had their electronics destroyed within minutes of landing. Traveling through the Van Allen belts once could kill the cosmonauts. A second time (on return from the moon) would kill them for sure.
Communications will improve over time, however at this stage we are experiencing many interference events. This makes it critically dangerous for manned missions as we

need to be in control of the craft at all times. If a problem arises and the cosmonauts cannot speak with ground control, then they will almost certainly perish.

Landing a large space craft on the Moon's surface has not yet been attempted and we have no means to address this today. Many of our small probes have crash landed and one that landed safely did not return to Lunar orbit. Even if it could be achieved, getting such a large craft to return to Earth orbit has too many negatives to even try at this stage of our work.

Rocketry has continued problems and trying to get enough thrust to lift a large space ship beyond Earth's gravitational control, will bring us many headaches to come. We are not ready. It is suggested by our science team that we may not be able to complete such a mission until the end of the 7th decade.

██████████████████

Chief Scientist
Manned Moon Mission

Clearly the Russians knew it was impossible to send men to the Moon without loss of life. And yet we did it? SEDA sent Lunar on a moon mission that the soviets had proven was impossible. So how on earth, did we do it? I have no evidence now to prove that the KGB passed this information on to the US. However, the Diaries are huge, and I am sure more evidence will come to light in the COMING WEEKS."

Later that night Cara and I went to meet Mel. It was strangely quiet around her apartment block. Something may be in the air, or my fear of being abducted again might be making me see ghosts. I was beginning to feel responsible for Hugo's death. It was like being the sole survivor of a natural disaster or a military campaign. Why was I alive, when I started this show?

Mel had been online most of the day. Gypsie was upstairs doing whatever Gypsie does. The most important piece of information we needed, was how did the Athena astronauts actually die: if they did at all. Mel was trying to get more documents from the Deep Web regarding finances. She believed that a money trail may lead to a cul-de-sac or a bulge in their defenses. That was a long shot. Even if we found this bulge, how were we going to determine what it meant? The only real way to introduce the misdirection to the people of the US and the world, was to write a story on the Athena mission. We all agreed that would be a good starting point and we could then feed the Diaries into it.

"On a cold but sunny morning at 0900hrs on the 16th day of July, the mightiest rocket ever built, lifted off the launch pad at Cape Kennedy. The massive Jupiter 5, standing taller than the Statue of Liberty, flawlessly took three American astronauts into history. Charlie Draper, Ed Robinson and Aaron Rosenbach, led the way on a mission to the future.

The ship was in three stages, the Command Module, named the Santa Maria after Christopher Columbus' ship, the Moon lander was called the Lewis, referencing the first exploration of the Western US by Lewis and Clark, and the Service Modules name was, well, the Service Module. The men on board had trained six years for this mission. They were all space rookies, trained especially for their decision making skills under pressure, shown in their careers as fighter jet test pilots. The only civilian on the mission was Charlie Draper, a retired Korean War hero, coaxed into SEDA's space program because of his hero status with the American public. If anyone could pull off this mission to the Moon, and unite the American people after a decade of political disasters, it was Charlie Draper.

After booster separation, the Santa Maria attached to the Service Module and the Lewis, orbited Earth on two occasions before 'go for TLI' (Translunar injection) was called from CapCom. Firing the main engines for a set time, controlled by the ships computer, saw the astronauts on their way to the Moon. The first human-beings to escape the gravitational orbit of the Earth and head off to a new world.

Three days later, Aaron Rosenbach, the Command Module pilot, fired a short rocket burst to put the Santa Maria and her cargo into Lunar orbit. To get into Luna orbit required the ship to slow down. This enable the Moon's gravity to capture the space ship and the speed at which the ship was traveling stopped it from crashing to the Moon's surface. Charlie Draper and Ed Robinson boarded the Lewis and disconnected from the mother ship. There was no turning back now. It was the Moon or bust! After the computer had controlled their descent to the surface of the Moon, the now famous radio message was heard.

'Longreach, Grissom Base here, the Lewis made touchdown! LONGREACH: Great news Charlie we can all breathe again...Lewis: Sure thing LONGREACH, we are go on all systems no warning lights over...LONGREACH: CM did you copy over.....CM: You betta believe it, I followed the whole thing, nice job boys...Lewis: Thanks Aaron...don't you go wandering off now, we may need a lift home!...CM: I'll make sure of that Charlie, nowhere to go the bars are closed.'

Draper and Robinson stayed a brief time on the Moon's surface, just long enough to plant the Stars and Stripes, gather some moon dust and end the first EVA on another planetary body in our solar system. After a well-deserved sleep, if that were even possible, the Lewis blasted off the Moon's surface and headed for Lunar orbit and re-docking with the Santa Maria. The job was done. They had made history and more importantly, had beat the Soviets to the Moon. America wins the Space Race.

Approaching Earth orbit, the Santa Maria shed both the Lewis and the service module. Re-entry had been successful on all US manned low Earth orbit missions. This would be a piece of cake: as they say in the classics.

'Longreach – CM, over'… CM this is LONGREACH'… 'LONGREACH we are go for re-entry over'… 'Roger, Aaron all systems are go here. Retro burnt in 5, 4, 3, 2, 1. Burn initiated. See you on the other side boys.' 'Roger LONGREACH.' 'LONGREACH – CM, picking up a blimp on the radar, closing fast… CM – LONGREACH 'we see it Aaron, may be a glitch'… ÇM its almost on us… it's hit! it's hit! We are out of control. May Day, May Day… shit we are in a steep descent, too steep. Getting hot in here, LONGREACH do you read?' 'CM read you 5 X 2. Can you get control over.' 'Negative LONGREACH, all controls are gone flames are flying past hugging the window, temp has risen to 55 Celsius, smoke in the cabin over.' … 'Shit, CM say again smoke over.'

By that time the CM had entered the no radio phase of re-entry. No matter how much Longreach tried to communicate with them, they were out of action until the module broke through to the lower atmosphere. By this time the whole world knew that the boys were in trouble and may not make it home. This had happened to the Russian's in the early days of re-entry but never to the US. What had they run into? What could be in space at that point and time? Only retrieving the Command Module would help answer those questions.

CapCom: 'There! There she is!' There were hundreds of millions of people watching on their TV sets. The US navy was waiting in the Pacific to retrieve the men and their ship. Everyone was tense. David Spitzer had seen the ball of flame hit the lower atmosphere. By now it should have no glow and definitely no flame. But it was streaming across the sky like a meteorite with a long tail of burning smoke. The fireball was Diariesed from North Carolina to Maine. That meant it was crashing on the eastern side of the US and the Navy was in a different ocean. Was it going to crash onto solid ground? That would mean no survivors. A search and rescue mission was launched centering on Katahdin Mountain, as the world's media was kept informed from Longreach. Mt Katahdin is 5,270 feet high at the end of the Appalachian Trail. It is rugged and remote and no-one could have foreseen such a disaster. A great crusade of journalist riding on their news agencies banners, headed for Longreach and Maine to cover, what was being touted as, America's greatest tragedy.

Mt Katahdin was pinpointed as the most likely source of impact. Of course no-one believed that there would be survivors. For now the game was recover the remains and examine the Command Module for possible clues. Was the Command Module really hit by space junk, a meteorite or a rogue satellite? It would be extremely difficult to tell. Fragments of the impactor would need to be found and analyzed to determine its origin.
Aircraft searches found the crash site late that morning and ground crews were choppered in. To the dismay of everyone, no reasonably intact bodies were found: just tangled clumps of metal and burnt human remains. The

remains were collected and returned to Longreach. After examination the identities of the astronauts were confirmed by the individual astronaut finger rings, and families began to grieve. Along with those heart broken families, the world shared their grief with a silence that could be felt. News telecast of the event quickly slowed, as media outlets considered it too much for the public to bare. Large celebrations that had been organized for the return of the 'Moon' men, were canceled, leaving empty chairs, tables, flags and streamers out in the open all over the US. We had won the space race but lost our infallibility."

Old Bridge

In the Warren, Wednesday afternoon, outside it was overcast and cold. The Warren was surprisingly warm, also dirty and strange. Belle had just contacted me, in regards to a location where she believed evidence of the Athena hoax was stored. We planned to meet in Old Bridge, New

Jersey, the next day at 8 am. She was going to show me an entrance to an underground ballistic missile silo used during the Cold War: long since disused and forgotten. Cara was going to see Teddy and then follow me, at a discreet distance. If she couldn't find him, she would text and make alternative arrangements. It was crucial for her that Teddy knows what she was doing, as he was the only link to clearing her name.

On arriving at Old Bridge I metup with Belle and started walking along what was Fort Hancock during the Cold War. It was situated on the narrow strip of heavily wooded land, which is ringed with beaches and jutted out six miles from the coast of Northern New Jersey, into the Atlantic Ocean, called Sandy Hook. I could see an old iron barbed wire fence surrounding a giant slab of concrete, which is partially hidden in layers of undergrowth. Faded yellow-painted markings are embedded into the floor. Old loudspeakers and disused arc lamps mark the perimeter. This was one of the most highly classified, top secret locations in the United States. Back in the day, if you were caught anywhere near it, the heavily armed patrols had orders to release their vicious attack dogs and shoot to kill on sight. Now mostly in ruins, these Cold War remnants were New York's last line of defense against Soviet nuclear attack [Spencer 2015]. Fort Hancock had become an historical district, frequented by tourists.

We made our way to the entrance of a concrete bunker. A sign in front of it said:
Extremely Hazardous Conditions: Area Closed

Belle did not know the exact place where this 'so called evidence' was. So I suggested we start at the base, some four stories down. There were no lifts and the stairs were a rusted metal construction of very dubious safety. I was guessing that if there was anything there, it must be well hidden because we had no problems finding the place.

Step by step was slow going with each new step tested before the next. Finally reaching the base of the bunker, where the air was foul and damp, we had a decision to make. There were four large tubular tunnels heading north, south, east and west. Splitting up was not an option. Not because I worried about belle's safety, it was more that I worried about mine, as I didn't really know who this Belle woman was. I could be walking to my own execution.

We headed north along a tube wide enough to take a train. After some 300 meters we were facing a T junction. Both ends of the T ended only a few meters in. One of them had a large metal and concrete door. The other looked like its door had collapsed. But in doing so, it had opened a small hole through the wall. 'I vote for this one', I said to myself and started to crawl through. Belle followed dragging her backpack after her.

Once inside it was easy to see that we had entered a huge concrete dome structure. In the center of the roof was a shaft that headed to the surface. It was allowing some light down to the floor. Everywhere there were metal and wooden crates. Rust, wood rot and tree roots had almost glued them all together. There was moss and strange weed type plants, with huge empty spider webs everywhere. I thought of Cara at this stage, and wondered where she was. I hadn't received a text message, so I could only assume she was watching somewhere up top.

Belle didn't really know what she was looking for. All she was told is that there was evidence here. But where? There were dozens of crates. Starting at the east side of the domed room, I began smashing open crates using a metal bar that was on the floor. Belle was taking photographs of the crates and the domed room. Me: 'leave me out of those Belle.' Belle: 'Why, I think you are very photogenic Mr. Virgil.' With a smile.

I continued smashing into the crates without a reply to that obvious come-on. All the crates seem to be filled with bits and pieces of rocket engines, unused electrical parts and other bits and bobs. Then at crate number six I found something interesting. Me: 'Better take a pic of this.' She came over and snapped a few shots. I started to poke around with the metal bar. What we were looking at seemed to be charred astronaut suits and lumps of burnt carbonized material.

Belle opened her 'magic' backpack and pulled out some baggies. That brought back some wild young Uni day memories. We took samples of the gunk and cloth. If this was evidence of Athena's astronauts, why was it dumped here? Surely these remains (if indeed they are remains) should have been buried in the shared grave at Arlington. A quick look about gave up no similar evidence. So now we had the long walk up and out of there. But hey, what about the other tunnels and especially the locked blast door. My investigative instincts took over and we were on a new path. After examining the inside of the dome chamber I found a small tight corridor similar to those in the Warren. So once more into the looking glass.

It was a tight squeeze through a narrow passageway that opened into a damp dark room. A quick scan with the torch light, showed a large pile of what appeared to be crates covered in tarps. Lifting one corner of a tarp exposed some small coffin sized metal trunks with padlocks. No problem with the padlocks, Belle picked them with a set of tweezers like thin tools. Now she was picking locks.

She lifted the lid. I was totally shocked. What an unexpected find. It was like a twist at the end of a good novel. Stacked four high, were Kalashnikovs wrapped in clear plastic: they were brand new. There must have been sixty trunks with each one holding 12 rifles and ammunition. That's seven hundred and twenty guns, maybe valued at $1,000.00 each minimum. WTF! Who owned these? They are not a relic of the Cold War, and the trunks still had shipping tags on them. This was a new cache and looked as though it hadn't been here long. If that were so, we may be in great danger. We came to get evidence for the Athena conspiracy, and have found ourselves caught up in the arms trade. Who owned these weapons? The Russian Mafia was known to deal in illegal weapons and I started to think that maybe I was standing near one of its operatives. Me: 'We have to leave, now!' Belle: 'Sure, just need to get a few more shots in.' I was up that shaky old ladder system like a rat up a drain pipe. I didn't want to be caught with this cache of murder tools. Along with a fresh bullet wound and my photograph on an FBI wanted list, it would be neigh impossible to talk my way out of this mess. And if the Russian Mafia arrived? Well I would be a dead man.

On reaching the top, I scanned for a vehicle. Where were Cara and Teddy? This find would be the path she needed to square herself with the Bureau. Me: 'I will need some of those images Belle. No-one is going to believe this without photo evidence.' She promised to send them via email as soon as she was back in Manhattan.   Once I was back at my hire car and Belle had vanished, almost literally, I broke protocol and sent Cara a text from my phone. Text to Cara: 'I have just found your saving grace. Fuck protocol babe call me. V.' I waited forty five minutes and no reply. Now I was worried. Time to get back to the Warren and onto the Deep Web.

Text to Cara: 'Where are you?' No reply. I was getting worried as Cara should have been at Sandy Hook or at least here at the Warren. I came in via the looking glass. I couldn't see any vehicles on the street that looked suspicious. Where were my minders? I tried Cara's phone again, and again. But no reply. I didn't have Teddy's phone number (don't know why not) so I Deep Webbed an SMS to Melanie. Melanie replied all most instantly. She wanted me to make my way to Dead Drop #2, so I headed off to Battery Park.

When I arrived Mel was already there. Strange that, she lived a good 30 minutes away. Melanie: 'Hi V. Let's walk.' So we went for a circumnavigation of Battery Park. Gypsie had been listing to NYPD phone traffic and had picked up an interesting call. Someone at the NYPD is talking with Teddy Rollins and the conversation was about Cara. Cara had been arrested after she contacted Teddy about the Sandy Hook trip. She had been taken to FBI headquarters in Lower Manhattan. Right where we were. Why wasn't Rollins arrested as well? Cara had contacted him so if the FBI were monitoring her phone, they would know who she was talking to and about what. That would mean that Teddy bloody Rollins would be in custody as well. But Gypsie had listened to him freely talking on his cell phone to someone at NYPD. It's beginning to look like mister bloody Teddy has turned against Cara.

I told Melanie about Sandy Hook and how Belle and I found hundreds of military grade weapons. Melanie was impressed and wanted to pass the info on to Anon: Rev. I question whether that was the smart thing to do, knowing that the Russian Mafia had no compassion for anyone that messed in their affairs. But hey, it's not my place to tell others what to do. Where have I heard that before?

I ask Melanie to thank Gypsie for me and to let her know that Cara had said the police can trace people scanning their phone systems. I worried for that girl. It would be a bad start to adulthood if she had a serious hacking charge against her. Melanie said not to be concerned as Gypsie was like a phantom on the WWW and with other technologies [clue]. So now I had to find Cara. I certainly couldn't rock up to the Bureau's headquarters and ask to speak with my girlfriend, whom they had recently arrested. And bloody Teddy was no good now as I was sure that he had knifed Cara: metaphorically speaking. My only choices were Anon: Revenge, or as a very last resort, Belle.

On the Deep Web I left message for anyone to try and find information on Cara Lucas. Next I contacted Belle. Using my cell phone direct was stupid but I was crazy with worried over Cara. Belle gave me a contact at the NSA. She said he would be able to help. Not that he could have Cara released, because that would be seen as being in collusion with whatever the Bureau thought Cara was involved in. But he could get a message to her and let me know if she was safe. OK, this was a big risk. Belle seemed to forget that I was also wanted. And the FBI would love to crucify the publisher of The Draper Diaries. But I had to do something, just sitting around waiting for an Anon to contact me was futile.

I phoned Belle's NSA contact, Antony Webb. Webb said he knew the case and that he would let me know what was happening later. To be safe I had called him from a public phone in Central Station. Of course he would know who I was and what was going down, but risk must be taken when a loved one or indeed a friend's safety is at risk.

Last year, when I was covering a story about a secret station beneath Grand Terminal, I was shown a door that led to Roosevelt's private train station. Inside was a large armored train carriage used to house FDR's limousine. It may seem as though I am wandering saying that, but it just goes to show what is happening beneath our very feet, without us ever knowing.

 It was way past time for another upload of The Draper Diaries. I didn't tell Webb about the weapons cache but later that day I saw on the news that the bunker had been raided. Two Russian Mafia criminals were arrested and the weapons seized. How did that happen? It could only be Belle. She has given me a name of an NSA officer and now the very secret weapons cache had been located. Is it just me or was Belle working for the NSA? I sent her a text asking for results from the gunk we gathered. 'As soon as I have them.' she replied.

The Truth News Online

August 4 2017

A Tomb of Lies

By Virgil Kaine

"In 1967 when the Santa Maria command module crashed into Katahdin Mountain, the official line was that very few body parts were found and that is why the remains were buried in one grave at Arlington. The Truth has information that there are artifacts from the Athena crash that have been stored underground in a secret location. And that these artifacts contain burnt human remains.

I traveled to this secret location with my source and together we examined the contents of some large crates, hidden four stories below the ground, under an abandon missile silo complex. Samples of the remains were taken and are now being examined by forensic experts. If these charred objects turn out to be the part of the remains of the Athena crew, then why wasn't they buried at Arlington? Was there any human remains buried at Arlington? Why were these remains stored in a hidden underground chamber?

SEDA has to answer these questions. Failure to say anything will be deemed as an admission of guilt to a crime or crimes not yet fully known. The Truth demands a reply from Rosealee Mishin. She has a duty to the families of the deceased astronauts and to the world at large. The Truth will not stop investigating the Athena mission, as every step we take in this private investigation unveils more questions. As soon as the results of the samples are known I will upload them to this news website."

There was a debate going on worldwide now, about freedom of speech, journalist rights, secrecy and national security. I guess that is a good spin-off but it isn't what I wanted. I want the media to concentrate on the Athena disaster, because that will open doors and force those involved to blink. And, when they do blink, like the stone angels of Doctor Who, we can surprise them.

Stranger than Fiction

The Truth News Online

August 5 2017

Lost in Space

By Virgil Kaine

"The Draper Diaries (the true account of the Athena Moon Landing)
The truth, so they say, is often stranger than fiction. Set yourself for a massive cover-up reveal. Everything you will read in this article is true and everything can be verified by other sources. The Truth News Agency is about to go down in history as the news agency that published the biggest historical lie in the history of human kind.

Not only will this shock the world it will also unlock a Pandora's Box of intrigue and confusion. This is the paramount story in US history. How a space agency, with or without government support, planned and executed a devious, murderous plot.

In 1967 SEDA launched a Jupiter booster rocket into low Earth orbit. It contained a command module (which the crew used) a lander module (for the moon landing) and a Service module that house all the electrics, water and oxygen. The astronauts were Charlie Draper (Commander Moon Lander), Ed Robinson (co-pilot Moon Lander) and Aaron Rosenbach (CM pilot).

They orbited the Earth three times before blasting out of Earth's gravitational hold and commenced their journey to the Moon. All seemed to be going to plan until half way through the Van Allen belts, all three men complained of nausea and headache. SEDA put that down to general space sickness and told the crew it would pass. It didn't.

Three days later the command module was orbiting the Moon at 100 miles out. The Lander module, which consisted of a descent module and an ascent module, was released from the CM after Draper and Robinson had made their way through the transfer hatch and donned their space suits. Flight suits were not considered suitable for the LM because they couldn't protect the astronauts from the vacuum of space. So the heavier spacesuits were worn complete with their own life support packs.

The LM was in a continuous melt orbit. This would allow it to be slowly dragged down towards the surface of the Moon. Their landing rocket, was a10,000lbs thrust single engine machine. It would be throttled back to less than 3,000lbs for the final landing stage. The LM had booster rockets that could be used to 'fly' the craft horizontally. As they came down through 18,000ft the rocket thrust was gradually throttled back.

'Lewis, this is Longreach over. Athena, Athena this is Longreach, do you copy over? (Static noises, gravelly broken voice) Ah say again Lewis. Longreach we are (static). CM, Longreach do you copy? Longreach CM, five by five. CM are you reading the Lewis? Negative

Longreach, no contact, maybe they are having another wiring issue, solar flare or something? CM can you see the Lewis? Negative! Longreach, I am 100 miles out! Can't see a thing, well, except the Moon. (Static noises)
CM - Longreach, change to secure comms, over? Roger Longreach.'
This was the recorded conversation, taped in Australia at the time the Lewis was said to be landing on the Moon. Totally different to the official release, which showed a smooth problem free landing. Now, the Truth is releasing the entire recording from Australia, taped in 1967.
'Roger Longreach.' CM this is Longreach, over. Longreach this is CM, send, over. Aaron we must get back in contact with the boys we want you to fire you reverse thruster on switch set AA. CM: OK Longreach, but that will get me to within 50 miles of the Lunar surface isn't that a bit low for the Santa Maria? Longreach: Negative Aaron, It will enable us to reconfigure your transceiver so we can get the boys up and running again. CM: Sure thing! In 5, 4, 3, 2, 1 - Burn initiated. Longreach: 3, 2, 1, shut down. CM: Roger shut down.

Once the comms were back up Longreach spoke to the Lander crew. Lewis this is Longreach, over. After a brief time of some static...Longreach this is Lewis, where's CapCom? Over. Longreach: He's on a brake would you believe it [clue] Sit Rep over. Lewis: We are down. Landed three minutes ago. Sorry you guys missed it. Everything appears OK, over. Longreach: Great job guys everyone here had their heart in their mouth when we couldn't reach you, over. Lewis: Better hearts then feet, over [clue].

LONGREACH: You are go for EVA, over. Lewis: All set just been waiting for your call, over.

Draper was the first astronaut to egress from the LM. At the base of the ladder he said, 'Really got no words for this maybe we should use the training tapes, over.' Lewis: Longreach you copy over? Longreach, over. Lewis this is CM over. Lewis: Hey Aaron where are those boys. I'm sick of these comms problems. CM: Longreach do you read over. Longreach: Sorry boys small glitch. The EVA was short and the astronauts were back in the LM getting ready to egress the Moon in the ascent module.

Lewis: Longreach we have a problem, over. Longreach: Send over. Lewis: You guys down there need to address this one fast. We can't re-compress the Landing Module, over. Static. Longreach: Working on it Charlie. Lewis: Make it quick we only have 45 minutes of O2 left. Longreach: Roger that.

If the ascent module could not be re-compressed, the astronauts would not be able to remove their spacesuits. Whilst they could still dock with the Santa Maria, they would not be able to transfer themselves to the command module, as the door opening between the two spacecraft was far too small for an astronaut wearing a spacesuit to pass through. They couldn't remove the spacesuit, because if they did, they would be in the vacuum of outer space. That meant, they would die!

CM: Longreach couldn't they dock and use the CM to recompress? Longreach: Negative CM, the Santa Maria doesn't have enough O2 to compress it, and the ascent module also.

Lewis: Well what the fuck! Are you going to do Longreach? We will die up here because of your incompetence! CM: They can't hear a word your saying Charlie. Lewis: I told those bastards that this might happen. No comms no answers! CM this is Ed, Charlie is right. Longreach doesn't give a shit, I bet you they are playing the practice tapes so the world thinks all is OK. CM: you really think so? Lewis: you better believe it Aaron. We can ascend but we need to get a plan in action so Charlie and I can move through the transfer hatch.

Longreach: Lewis, Longreach over. Lewis: Where the fuck have you been we have less than 45 minutes of O2 we have to egress the moon and dock with Aaron, at least then we have a chance. Longreach: Roger that Charlie, the boys are working flat here. I have a dozen engineers working on the problem. Lewis: well get a dozen more for Christ sake! Longreach: Lewis you are go to ascent over. Lewis: Roger that!

The Lewis fired the ascent engine and blasted off the landing module. They were traveling at the required feet per second to reach the command module. At 18,000 feet the ascent engine cut off. Lewis: Longreach the ascent engine has stop! Can't restart. Another bloody electrical fault. Urgent assistance is now required! Longreach: Lewis fire retros over. Lewis: firing now. No go Longreach we are losing altitude. We are doomed you bastards!

There was no reply from Longreach they had cut communication channels. Only the command module had secure comms. CM: Longreach they are plummeting towards the surface. They will both die! Longreach: Sorry Aaron we have no way to restart the engine from here.

Don't look. You don't want that memory. CM: It's done. They are down. No blast? The fuel should have exploded on impact [clue]. We have to tell the world what happened. Charlie and Ed are heroes and everyone should know. Are you receiving Longreach? Longreach this is CM over. Longreach, Longreach this is Aaron over.

That's when the transmission ended. Aaron Rosenbach was left alone 50 kilometers out from the Moon watching the destruction of the LM and his pals. The next transmission was the SOS from deep space. " SOS to the World SOS they have murdered me." Alfonso Cipriani had tested the origin of that Morse code SOS message. It came from beyond the Moon. If Aaron Rosenbach had been left in a decaying Moon orbit, he would have shared the same fate as the Landing Module crew. However, the SOS came from deep space beyond the moon. Why? And, what was the re-entry story all about. If Draper and Robinson died on the Moon, how could they also die on re-entry into the Earth's atmosphere three days later?"

Have I used the phrase 'shit hit the fan' before? Because it did, in no uncertain way. The White House cried false news and had the Truth's website blocked by a special sitting of the high court, late that night. We were dead in the water, as they say in the classics. The only way to get the news out now was to use Anonymous. Mel was my only safe contact. I found out from her that there was going to be a 'free Cara Lucas' sit-in at Battery Park. That's not far from the FBI headquarters. I intended to go once I could get my hands on a Guy Fawkes mask.

I went to Battery Park. It was beginning to feel like a second home. I expected about 20 people to turn out, one with a loudhailer maybe. But to my great surprise and comfort, there must have been 2,000 Guy Fawkes' standing silently in Battery Park. This was a peaceful protest and the media were out in force. There were hastily made placards saying 'FREE CARA LUCAS' and that brought a lump to my throat. Just about everyone there wouldn't have met Cara, and yet here they were protesting her arrest. Melanie and I found each other by text messages. She told me that Rev had organized the event in only a few hours. I was beginning to love that guy!

Part Two: Thus Always To Tyrants

Vasily

Vasily Khovanski is believed to be a Russian diplomat and spy coordinator and some sources say he has links with the mafia. He was posted to the Russian consulate in New York City just three months ago. I am not clear how he knows Liberty Belle, but they seem close. I am aware that he is under investigation by multiple US agencies. However, Khovanski has strong ties with political muscle and it will be difficult for the US law enforcement agencies to pin him down. If indeed he has links with Russian organised crime, then he will most likely be a player in the Moscow Mafia.

The Moscow Mafia are named after the Black Sea port city of Odessa, they are a key organised crime body trafficking in post-Soviet military arms: something that Khovanski could get his hands on. They also sell Europe-bound Afghan heroin arriving from the Caucasus. Even in Russia's east, gangs are often closely involved in the lucrative trafficking of heroin, people, and counterfeit cigarettes into Europe, often in cooperation with Russian mafia gangs. In the US they have been closely associated with gun running to Mexico.

Odessa traditionally had an ancient culture of banditry, dating back to the large and impoverished Jewish population. Famous writers such as Isaac Babel often wrote about the infamous exploits of Jewish gangsters, thieves and crime lords in the port city. Twentieth century thuggery made way for sophisticated organised crime when local crime lords began to use the city's sprawling port to their advantage. At first, the locally active Moscow Mafia, sometimes who are also known as the Malina, [strange that][clue]became well known when it branched out to New York City and later to Israel. Many people from Moscow's Jewish population migrated abroad, among them a large part of the city's most infamous career criminals. Although the gang was born in the city of Moscow, it has since established most of its headquarters in places such as New York City, Tel Aviv, Antwerp and Budapest, with brigades composed of former Moscown or Moscow connected criminals active elsewhere.

In the United States the Moscow Mafia is based in the Brighton Beach district of Brooklyn, New York. It is regarded as the most powerful post-Soviet criminal organisation in the USA and has since expanded its operations to Los Angeles, where it has established connections with locally based Armenian and Israeli crime figures. It's known for being a very secretive organisation, being involved in protection rackets, loan-sharking, murder-for-hire, as well as the infamous fuel tax fraud rackets and narcotics trafficking.

Nonetheless, a large amount of Moscow Mafia-connected gangsters have become part of the US criminal folklore, examples being Marat Bilingual, Evsei Agron and Boris Nayfeld. Feuds often resulting in extreme violence, happened in the 1980s and 1990s between Moscow Mobsters such as the internal war between Balagula and

Agron at first, and later on between the Nayfeld brothers and Monya Elson.

Following the collapse of the former Soviet Union, there were large stockpiles of arms left in Ukraine. The first prominence of the Moscow Mafia came through their participation in the illicit international trafficking of these arms. Between 1992 and 1998, some $32 billion in military material disappeared from military depots in Ukraine and ended up primarily in West Africa and Central Asia. Allegedly, Moscow criminal organisations were also behind trafficking weapons to war-torn places such as Afghanistan at the time.

From trafficking in arms, Moscow crime syndicates entered into the international trade in illegal drugs, becoming a major player in the narcotics traffic from Central Asia to Central Europe. The reach of gangs has become extended, having been Diariesed from Central European countries such as the Czech Republic and Hungary, where they're involved in prostitution, to North American countries and Israel, where they founded a significant power base following the mass immigration of Ukrainian Jews, which among the many law-abiding people, there were also criminal elements profiting from the open borders [Wikipedia_3].

At Sandy Hook Belle and I found a cache of Russian military weapons. These must belong to the Moscow mafia in Brighton Beach. I suspect if we have have searched further, we may have found much more. I am inclined to return and check, but it will be dangerous. Now that the cache is in the hands of the ATF (the Bureau of Alcohol,

Tobacco, Firearms and Explosives) the owners may be looking for payback. I believe Belle told the ATF where the cache was. Yet if the owners are Russian, she knows the Russians, so why would she blow the whistle on them? But also she is so bloody secretive. I can't really join the dots yet.

Why has a media investigation into the Athena moon shot got me involved with the Moscow mafia? It just doesn't make sense. I knew I had to go back and check the silo bunker, no matter what the cost, because there was a strong link between the Athena mission data in The Draper Diaries and the Moscow Mafia.

When I arrived at the site on Sandy Hook, there were no police cars. OK, that's a good start. A police tape was stretched across the bunker entrance. I looked down the shaft and once again into the looking glass. I was met with the cold damp air that seemed to hang rather than circulate. Straight-up I returned to the cache room and found that every metal trunk had been removed. That was some feat! How did they get them up the shaft? The structure is seriously corroded and dangerous. Maybe there is a way out from one of the tunnels. I could see foot prints in the moist dirt that had settled on the base of the tunnels over the years. So I followed them with much trepidation as I could be walking to my death.

The tunnel led to another domed room that was cleaner than the rest of the complex. There was a door that had a large hanging padlock. No problem I thought, because I brought along a sturdy length of two inch steel. I put the steel inside the upturned U of the padlock and twisted it back and forth until it broke the lock. On entry there was a railway cart on tracks that led to a shaft. The shaft was a solid construction and had a set of hoist wire ropes hanging from the top. Where did that go? I was assuming that it came out in one of the old buildings on the surface. So back up top to check that out.

When I reached the surface I was startled by an old homeless guy. He said that he had information about the silo if I would pay him. Oh yeah where have I heard that one before. Me: 'If you tell me something useful, then I'll pay.' Hobo: 'Well, I saw them boys take out a large metal looking frisbee thinge.' Me: 'A frisbee?' Hobo: 'Yeah that's what I said are you deeth?' Me: 'Can you describe it a little better than that, like size color etcetera.' Hobo: 'Yeah, it was about 5 to 6 feet wide and was grey in color. One side was flat and t'other was like a little hill.' Me: 'Which way did they go?' Hobo: 'dun know, but the truck said Longpeach or some-thin like that.' Me: 'Longreach.'

I paid him enough for breakfast and a coffee and I guess a bottle of something. He seemed happy with that. God, he needed to take a shower more often. He smelt like a dead animal. The frisbee shape sounded very much like a command module heat shield. WTF was a heat shield doing down there? Hidden in the same area as illegal guns, that may be owned by the Moscow Mafia. Some images were beginning to grow in my mind.

When I got back to the Warren, with a bite to eat. I setup my cell phone aerial and sent a text to Belle. I asked her if she had heard anything about Cara yet, as I had no word from her NSA man. She said that she hadn't but that wasn't a bad thing necessarily. And, that I should contact her every day for updates. I really was worried about my girl. I got her into this and now I had to get her out. Belle gave me a message from Khovanski to meet him in Central park (again with the bloody parks) today at noon. It was 11:45AM. Into a Yellow and up to the park.

Khovanski was leaning against a tree talking on his cell phone. We made the usual small talk greetings then went for a stroll. I asked him what was all this about and why did the Russians have so much interest in what I am doing? Khovanski: 'It's not so much what you are doing Mr. Virgil, it is more the end result of accumulative effects. My job is not an easy one. I have to give consular assistance to Russian citizens here in USA. But it doesn't stop there. We are concerned by the amount of illegals in Brooklyn that are associated with the Moscow Mafia. One of my tasks is to gather information about these illegals and pass it on to US law enforcement. Russia does not want these mafia criminals from establishing a solid base here in USA because, they ultimately project their crime and successes to Moscow. We, have an arrangement with US law enforcement agency. We help them and they help us. It's, how you say, symbiotic.'

Well did I believe that crap? Not one bit of it. This was designed to put me on side with him so I would pass on information. He must think I am a cadet journalist. Me: 'I have one concern Vasily. What connection is there between the Athena moon landing and the Russian Government?' Khovanski: 'Russia wants to clear name. We were blamed for Athena crash. We did nothing to Athena. Our technology was behind USA. But everyone in world thought we did it. Now the cost is still current. Our relationship with USA should be much better. Russians are not communist. We like USA, money drives our economy not ideology. So Russia wants you, Mr. Virgil, to expose SEDA and help to clear our name.'

It is not that long ago that he appealed to me to back off from publishing The Draper Diaries. Now he is in favor of them. The more he talked the more I didn't believe him. But some of it may be true. At this stage my mind was more set on getting Cara free.

Khovanski: Oh, by the way Mr. Virgil. I hear your Cara is been arrested. Maybe consulate can help.' I didn't reply. He walked off towards the Zoo. Maybe he fucking lived there. I was getting mighty pissed off with this whole affair. How was he going to intervene on Cara's behalf? He wasn't a US citizen. But Belle has contacts and I needed to press her more about Cara.

The Truth News Online

August 6 2017

Guns, Guns and More Guns

By Virgil Kaine

"Strange things can happen from time to time, when investigating one possible crime, another turns up that appears to be unrelated and then has links to the first, making the show bigger and more dangerous. All you good law abiding citizens out there, may not know much about the resident Russian Mafia here in New York. There are places that have become 'home away from home' for organized Russian criminals.

Drugs and illegal firearms are the money spinners here in the US for the biggest 'Russian' mafia group, the Moscow gang. After the US media blamed the Russians for the deaths of Draper, Robinson and Rosenbach in 1967, there was a push to enter the US and create havoc via organized crime. Anon: Revenge, has uncovered links to immigration consultants and the desire to 'burn' America in the fires of criminal activity.

This is not hard to believe when we consider that everyone who feels aggrieved wants some form of payback. Magnify that by a nation's population and you have the roots and the capacity, to deliver payback on a large sustainable level.

A new player has emerged as the prime mover of the Moscow gang. His name is not known, however he goes by the code name 'New Tarzan' and is believed to be active in NYC at this very time. This invasion of Russian criminals, may have started as a payback tactic for the Athena accusations, but now it is a pure world of organized crime. They have no alliance to the Space Race of the past. Their aim is to circumvent law enforcement anywhere in the world, so they can continue their money making rackets with impunity.

The Draper Diaries has no mention of organized crime in the modern sense. However, it does house documents that can point US law enforcement in the right direction, to enable them to combat these foreign criminals.

Lazarus

Sneaking back into the Warren was becoming a pain, not just for the inconvenience but for my lower back as well. Setting up my phone I got a message from Belle saying that Cara was being released today. WTF how did that happen? Surely not Khovanski? At any rate I waited anxiously for her return. Not knowing where she was being held, I couldn't go and meet her. I went upstairs to the Ranch so I could keep watch from the front windows. Just in case Cara tried the Warren I left a note.

Cell Phone Call Mel: 'Verge, Gypsie has found some information that Cara is being released today.' Me: 'Yeah that's right, great ah.' Melanie: 'Really good Verge. Gypsie also said, a friend of hers has been watching FBI headquarters and saw Cara leave with Teddy.' Me: 'OK if he comes here I will have strong words with bloody Teddy.

Then the front door opened and in walked my girl, complete with sadness and a smile at the same time. I love hugs. We hug all the time. When we greet we hug. When either says something good or funny, we hug. We have a huggy relationship. Cara had been held in Lower Manhattan but only interviewed early this morning. Strange that? Why would they park her in a cell and do nothing with her until today? I asked questions and she gave answers but really there wasn't much to say about the ordeal. Then I told her about the arms cache, Belle and Khovanski. Cara was not convinced that Belle, whom she now called Malina, was a Russian spy, or if she was, she is a double agent working with the NSA. No matter what she didn't want me to trust Khovanski: Roger that.

The immediate problem now was to make sure we didn't run from the fry pan into the fire, by letting the Moscow gang get us. They have already murdered Hugo, abducted me and threatened Cara's life. The stakes were high though because we had two tasks now. The first, publishing the rest of The Draper Diaries and the second, investigating the Moscow mafia and any possible links to Athena. After-all, I can just hear Hugo saying; 'It's all good news and the press is a free agent.' And protected by the 1st Amendment I spoke to myself.

Cell text Msg from Gypsie?: 'V REV wants you to logon to Deep Web, now!' Reply: 'Gypsie? What are you doing? Stay out of this mess!' No response.

Deep Web Chat Site Anon-Hermes: 'REV where are you?' Anon-Revenge: 'Hermes, I have a new contact. Code name Boilerplate. He was onsite during Athena re-entry. Has been laying low for 50 years, now after reading the Diaries he wants to add to the content. Says he has a bombshell to give.' Anon-Hermes: 'Great REV! Where, when, how?' Anon-Revenge: 'Sandy Hook. Tomorrow at 8am.' Anon-Hermes: 'OK will be there. And thanks man.' Anon-Revenge: ;-)

Arriving at Sandy Hook, Cara and I surveyed the landscape for possible tails and to find this Boilerplate. Sandy Hook was a lot of ground to find someone so we hope he would show himself to us, rather than us trying to find him. Text from Belle: 'Go to the light house.' Me: 'OK.'

We drove to the light house and saw an elderly man sitting in a car smoking a cigarette. Cara: 'That will be him V.' Me: 'Yup.' We walked over to him and introduced ourselves. He looked older than he probably was, or at least weathered. Given his involvement in Athena, I guessed he would have been in his twenties then. He wanted to show me where bodies were buried under the floor of the very same silo where Belle and I had found, what we thought were Human remains. But he knew an easier way to get there. One of the buildings had a set of stairs under its floor that led to the silo base. They looked well maintained and were made of timber and metal. So, down we went.

This Boilerplate guy didn't seem to have much of a problem getting down the stairs but I wondered how was he going to get back up? Our little Lewis and Clark expedition made its way to the base of the missile silo. Me: 'Hey you know that this was full of crates last week.' Boilerplate: 'I know, I helped put them there.' He scratched out a square in the middle of the concrete floor with a screw driver. Me: ' Mate they were Moscow guns, what is your connection there.' Boilerplate: 'It's a very long story maybe some other time. Under here, there are three bodies, they were burned in a command module and dropped over Mt. Katahdin from a B52 bomber. You have to get this dug up so the truth can be known.'

I agreed and we took photographs and some measurements. Then we headed out. But instead of climbing the stairs we went to where I had broken the door padlock. Boilerplate put his left hand into a large wide crack in the wall. I could feel Cara's heart beat race. He pushed a hidden switch and a platform elevator descended to the floor.

Me: 'Why didn't we come down this way.' Boilerplate: 'The switch only works from the bottom. There is no switch up top.' Once on the surface he told us to follow him to his house in Middleton Township.

He lived in what I can only say was a very modest dwelling, in need of some TLC. It had a large front window set out from a veranda on both sides. It couldn't have been any wider than 18 feet. It had been painted sky blue back in its day. Now it was a case of a house with a flaking dermis. On entry, the conditions were not much better. This is a guy who lived on almost nothing. A Spartan life, which seemed too harsh for an old man [clue]. We sat and chatted about his past work at Longreach. I did asked him what his name was but he refused to tell me: another Belle I thought to myself. He had been following The Draper Diaries in the Truth and wanted to add to the story while he still had the chance. We agreed to have an interview and that I would tape it and publish it on the Web.

The Truth News Online

August 7 2017

Boilerplate

By Virgil Kaine

"Interview with code name boilerplate.

The following is the transcript of an interview conducted by yours truly, with a man from the 1967 Athena program, code named Boilerplate (I refer to him as BP).

Me: 'BP, would you explain who you are, at least as far as you can. Considering the secrecy involved.'

BP: 'I was a part of the Athena Moon mission program in 1967. Since then I have lived the life of a recluse.'

Me: 'Why did you contact the Truth News Agency?'

BP: 'I have been following your articles and I knew you needed more than it appeared you had. So I contacted you.'

Me: 'You know that many people will reject what you have to say because they will not believe you. Not knowing who you really are. So why can't you tell me your real name?'

BP: 'Because if I did, many people would be effected in ways that would be cruel to them. So it is better this way. Your readers will have to put two and two together. I can only tell you what I know.'

Me: 'What was your job on the Athena program?'

BP: 'No I can't tell you that.'

Me: 'Did Draper and Robinson land on the Moon in 1967?'

BP: 'Yes.'

Me: 'And Rosenbach stayed in the command module?'

BP: 'that's right, only two astronauts could land. The third had to keep the command module in orbit ready for the re-docking and the return journey home.'

Me: 'Did they see stars either on the way to the Moon or on the Moon.'

BP: 'Stars, in space?'

Me: 'Yes.'

BP: 'I can't really say. On Earth we knew just as much as you know now. They never talked about stars.'

Me: 'You say the USA did land on the Moon, so why do we have this conspiracy movement and why do you think Anonymous and the Russians are involved?'

BP: 'Not too many questions at once ah, I am an old man and although I have a good memory my CPU is slow.'

Me: 'Sure.'

BP: 'To answer your questions in reverse, the Russians or Soviets at the time, [we] can't blame people who were not born then, had an agreement with the US over the space race. The idea was that without some form of massive spending over a period of at least a decade, both countries would be economically weakened to such a point, that the Leader of either one, may press the button.'

Me: 'The atomic bomb you mean?' BP: 'Yes, that's right. Poverty breeds revolution and neither country wanted that. And certainly the entire Cold War was a mockery of reality. We would never have made a 'First Strike' and neither would they. But that doesn't create jobs on its own. You can only build so many war machines before the public rise up in protest. The answer was to create a Space Race that had all the fervor of beating each other to the Moon and yet, was benign. So what started out as a real race for military dominance soon collapsed into a stage play.

Me: 'And the Anonymous?" BP: 'I have no idea really. They are not from my generation and the technologies have left me for dead. Who knows?' Now the first part of your question, why is there a moon hoax movement, can be answered in two parts. Firstly, I sowed the first seed of doubt. Not publicly, but among my friends and coworkers. It has been built from there. But the other side is that, in these more modern times, conspiracies are popular and many books have been written about the Moon Hoax. I have read them all. Most of them are wrong. But some are right on the money.

Me: 'Were parts of the Athena mission faked?' BP: 'Absolutely. There was a perceived idea that something may go wrong and if it did we did not want the enemy or our own people seeing it. When I say we, I mean the US.' Me: 'Right.' With a nod. BP: 'At first it was suggested to just do a fake moon landing film, and have it ready just in case of radio communications problems or a crash. Now I was only aware that these films were made for training purposes and were never intended to replace reality. Unfortunately they did.

Me: 'When were you first aware of the fakes being used?' BP: 'I can't tell you that. That would endanger innocent people.' Me: 'OK so you still think that SEDA would hurt other people?' BP: 'No not SEDA, SASS! They were the guard dogs across the isthmus. They watch our every move. You see, we were a civilian organization, aiming for the stars. SASS were/are a military security organization that was embedded with SEDA to monitor and protect Cold War achievements. When there seemed to be a comms problem with the Lewis, I was told via my headset to switch to rehearsed scripts and answer the incoming voices, with the replies in those scripts. Of-course when we did the scripts it was said, that they were a method to get us used to communicating and to help us smooth out our voices. I had no idea really that they would be used.

Me: 'So was the radio signal picked up in Australia real?' BP: 'Oh yes, it was the point that I lost comms with the

Lewis and the Santa Maria and used scripted reply's. Me: 'So what did happen that day 250,000 miles out from home?' BP: 'Well, Charlie and Ed landed on the Moon. No-one on Earth saw the real landing. Then after they did a brief EVA, they were getting ready to have their sleep before take-off the next day. But to sleep they needed to get out of their spacesuits and to do that, the landing module cabin had to be re-pressurized with an atmosphere. But it didn't work. The cabin pressurization failed. Time and time again. Longreach did not know what to do. And I think now that their plan was always to leave the crew on the moon and fake the rest.

Me: 'But that would mean not trying to save them, maybe manslaughter and who were the three men that died on re-entry?' BP: 'Oh, before we get to that. Charlie and Aaron [Rosenbach] decide to try and get the Lewis into orbit and then dock the two space craft. But they wouldn't be able to move between the ships because the guys in the Lewis had to leave their spacesuits on, complete with life support backpacks. Now, that was risky. Aaron wanted to pump air from the Santa Maria to the Lewis once they were connected. But Longreach over-ruled that decision, stating that, the Santa Maria would decompress as well and then they would all die. Me: 'Why didn't Rosenbach just do it?' BP: 'You can't do anything in those ships without Longreach approval. Longreach had remote control of both craft.' Me: 'So what really happened?'

BP: 'The boys tried to ascend to Lunar orbit as they didn't want to die on the Moon. But the ascent modules rocket fuel ran out at 18,000 feet. They spiraled back down to the surface and crashed. Aaron witnessed it all and became very upset. At this stage Longreach cut comms completely.' Me 'You are telling us that Charlie Draper and Ed Robinson crashed and died on the Moon. Is that right?' BP: 'Totally. They are still there. And that's why we have never gone back. If we did, the cat would be let out of the bag and all hell would brake lose.' Me: 'So what happened to Rosenbach?' BP: 'Aaron's fate is unknown to me. All I can say is the recording picked up by Alfonso Cipriani, must have been Aaron. Longreach most likely tried to get him back. But knowing Aaron, he would have screamed bloody murder when he got home. So my guess is that he was rocketed remotely into a heliocentric orbit of the Sun, where he had four days of oxygen before he would die' Me: 'Meaning?'

BP: 'The Santa Maria would orbit the Sun at some prescribed distance from Earth, forever. Aaron too, is still out there.' Me: 'Can you tell me what happen on re-entry to the Earth's atmosphere and who those men were?' BP: 'The answer to that took me quite a while to find out. But hold on to your cell phone. SASS hatch a plan over the three days it would have taken the boys to return from the Moon. They abducted three homeless men from uptown New York. They were placed in a boilerplate command module…' Me: 'what is a boilerplate?'

BP: 'A boilerplate is something that is not functional but for all intent and purpose looks real. We had several boilerplate CMs and used them for training exercises. It is believed that those poor bastards were gassed with cyanide when they were strapped into the CM seats. Seats, by the way, that would not have fitted them because they were individually made to the shaped of each astronaut's body, when lying on their back, even the mock seats.' Me: 'How did they get them into orbit when I can't find any information stating that there was another Jupiter launch at that time?' BP: 'Easy! They never went into orbit. They were first burnt in situ, and that has caused me 50 years of nightmares, and then dropped from a B52 over the wilderness in Maine. That's as much as I know, or, can tell you.

That is an accurate transcript of our interview with the mysterious Boilerplate. The evidence that he has given would be enough to send any individual to prison for the rest of their days. It shows that the Soviet Union cannot and should not be blamed for the deaths of Draper, Robinson and Rosenbach. Why? Because those heroes are still on the Moon and orbiting in deep space. Preserved forever. One day they will be found. But will the astronauts and the three unknowns get justice? That remains to be seen."

Bloody Teddy

I should have stayed home that day. Our interview with Boilerplate went viral and caused massive unrest here in the US. Manhattan was in railway lock-down as Anonymous staged a sit-in. Not at the familiar Battery Park but across the train tracks under Central Terminal and Union Square. There were more than 50 of these guys and girls all wearing Guy Fawkes masks. REV had set it up to protest at the lack of government action after Boilerplate's evidence was aired on YouTube. It created huge delays and saw the NYPD storm the underground in force. There were 21 arrests and 13 injured in the process.

However, that was light compared to the fracas in Verona, NJ. An estimated 200 individuals marched on the Longreach SEDA building. Many wearing, what we're becoming, the Anon mask, and many more with their faces covered with anything they could find. They were loud and angry, voicetress and agitated by the shocking news on our YouTube video.

The protest (later referred to as a riot) began like most do: peacefully. However after protesters refused to leave the compound of the SEDA, arrest began. This caused others to try and save their friends and allies. For some time it was open warfare in the streets and car parks of Verona. Paramedics were brought in and they treated many of the injured. However, the Anonymous kept protesting. They regrouped and headed for the SEDA's main building's front entrance. There was no way that the local police could control them. Their numbers seemed to swell by the minute as busloads of protesters arrived. Placards called for the SEDA director to be jailed and SEDA to be shut down. To be fare though, Rosealee Gregorio is only 52 years old, so she can't be blamed for the actions of others 50 years ago.

The media were arriving in force, which only spurred the Anons to greater heights. The front doors of SEDA were smashed in and the security guards assaulted. I felt sorry for them. The protesters were beaten back by a contingent of SASS, FBI like officers.

In the meantime, the Major of Verona had called for National Guard assistance. It was granted and soon there were 200 soldiers disembarking from trucks and troop carriers. A little over the top I thought but it made great press. The National Guard lined up in some form of military arrangement and stormed the 'mob', as I heard their commander call the protesters. Well it wasn't pretty. The NG had batons and used them with gusto. The protester broke ranks and ran into an oncoming Anon reinforcement. With the NG laying out rough justice behind them and the new Anons busting to get into the fight, many were injured in a crush of flesh and boots.

 Two protesters were shot by someone farther back in the shadows. As of today no-one knows who fired the shots. Maybe a nervous National Guard member. For me I can't go past a SASS officer trying to get some personal payback and incite more violence. I got out in the confusion and made my way back to the Ranch. I couldn't stomach the Warren tonight.

The next night Cara had a text from bloody Teddy. I ask her why she still trusted that bastard. She said she didn't but she knew what she was doing and who she had to protect. Cara: 'I am on a bit of a leash V, I've got to see it through.' I decided to come as backup. I'll stay in the dark and keep watch. Cara gave me a colt 45 that she kept in her bits and pieces drawer. I wasn't all that good with guns but she had given me lessons about a year ago.

Cara met bloody Teddy in Central Park. They talked for a while and I kept my distance. Then I noticed someone walking, in a manner of urgency, toward them from 5th Avenue. It was so quick I couldn't believe my eyes. The light flashes came first and then the bang X 2 of a gun. The 'intruder' fell forward and Cara screamed No! That was enough for me, I took off towards Cara at breakneck speed. She was on the ground huddled over the person shot. Bloody Teddy was standing there waving his gun and babbling something. Cara turned towards him half crouched and screamed at him. She instantly reminded me of DiCaprio's portrayal of Romeo as he shot Tybalt. It is now burnt into my mind.

Cara: 'You killed her you bastard! You murdered her.' BT: 'No-No she is Anon: Revenge! I had to it's my job, just like it is yours!' Cara was red with rage and lifted her gun and fired while screaming at him. One, two, three, four shots, before he fell. I had only just reached her then. She dropped the glock and fell into my arms trying to restrain the anguish she felt inside her. I looked over to the dead woman lying on ground, as I held Cara. I could she who was shot. She wasn't moving and there was no sign of breathing.

I really was numb when I saw Melanie lying face down on the pavement. Cara was quietly crying and I had a heavy sinking painful feeling in my chest, and my mouth went dry. I checked Melanie's vitals and found no pulse. She had been shot right through the lower sternum and on into the heart. There was no point in trying to save someone who is not biologically savable, even though first respondents try it all the time, for me, it's disrespectful. We couldn't save her nor could we stay with her because, this would see us locked up for a very long time. Coupled with all the riots and the Truth articles it doomed us. I couldn't see a way out. Somehow I had to tell Gypsie. But How? My heart sank.

Gypsie

Although Gypsie was only 15 years old, she is far from a child. She is very independent and has a unique kindness that is rare. She is sad within herself and this has lead to long hours on her own. Surfing the internet, especially the dark web was her way of fulfilling what she didn't have. Gypsie was an independent, somewhat shy person with an advanced intellect. No-one would play chess for money with her. She had advanced planning skills and could retain chess moves with aforethought.

In order to see her we couldn't go to her apartment, because it wouldn't take long for the NYPD to find out who poor Mel and bloody dead Teddy were. So I sent her an SMS from the Deep and told her to meet me behind the MET. To stay low and quiet. Typically she replied: 'Whatever V.' Any sign of adventure would have Gypsie on the move. When she arrived we moved on to get a Yellow and back to the Ranch. I told Gypsie we had important information for REV, and we needed to get home to show her. Lies I know, but what else could I say? I certainly wasn't going to tell her in the street that her mother had just been gunned down by a rogue FBI agent who was probably working for the Moscow mob.

Before entering the Warren through the looking glass, Cara checked the surroundings. She was still visibly traumatized. Then we did the usual bend and crawl movement to get into the Warren without being seen. Gypsie was in her element. Luckily, this was a quiet area which allowed us to detect if we were being watched. I felt concerned for Gypsie but Cara as well. Fear of spiders is not like losing your mother, but hey, it's damn awful and she was now very vulnerable.

I don't really know how to write this next piece. Telling a 15 year old that her mother has just been murdered is not an easy task. Gypsie has the right for her emotions to be kept private. Suffice to say, it was traumatic and gut retching. Both Cara and I cried along with Gypsie in our embrace. She wanted to see her mother. Of course this was impossible. We had no idea how it was going to play out. Even Gypsie may be in danger of arrest for scanning police frequencies. I just wasn't prepared to take the risk. But as I should have guessed, knowing Gypsie, she bolted. I knew that she would head back to the 5th Ave apartment. That's where she lived and that's where she would feel her mother's presence.

Cara was quick to respond and took after Gypsie. Modern girls have their own money and Cara saw her get into a Yellow. So she followed discretely in another. Don't really know whether she said 'follow that taxi', no that's dumb, just my stupid mind overheating. Cara left the Yellow one block before the apartment and ran the rest of the way. Gypsie was about to walk through the front door of the complex, when Cara grabbed her arm. There was a brief struggle, before poor Gypsie slumped to the ground crying loudly. Cara had to get her away from there. There were two FBI vehicles parked just around the corner, so the chance that the apartment was being searched was high. Maybe they were waiting for Gypsie to return, either way, Cara had to convince Gypsie to return to the Warren. I was busily writing my next column when they returned. Cara wanted to take Gypsie upstairs to the Ranch. There were no facilities in the Warren. So we all egressed the sandstone and brick maze. In the broken Ranch Cara set Gypsie up in the bedroom and stayed with her for the night. My aim was the same as always: get another column online. I worked in the bathroom so I didn't have to switch the lights on in the living room. The bathroom light couldn't be seen from the street. After forty minutes or so I had the column finished.

The Truth News Online

August 8 2017

An Open letter

By Virgil Kaine

"Since the Truth published its first article on The Draper Diaries, trouble has come our way. Our family and friends have been subjected to abuse, assaults and sadly, in two cases now, death. I place the blame for all events, including the deaths of Hugo Kent and Melanie Illingworth squarely on the shoulders of SEDA. There has been no word from the government since Boilerplate's interview. He gave damning evidence in regard to murder and deceit by SEDA's security division, SASS. Where are the rebuttals? Where are the leaders condemning his interview? Silence in a court of law can be seen as guilt and cowardice. And silence in the public arena, shows the same white feather.

The issues that have arisen in The Draper Diaries are as follows:

- The Morse code message picked up by Cipriani in Italy,
- The SOS to the world from deep space.
- Australia's radio signal tapes and the Moon landing problems.
- Issues of safety with the Lunar Excursion Module.
- Broad ranging cover-ups of disaster and plots.
- Hugo Kent's bashing in Manhattan.
- The mention of three unknown men allegedly murdered by SASS. Why hasn't SASS come forward?
- The fake moon landing photographs.
- Soviet cover-ups in league with the US.
- The outright re-entry lies from 1967.
- Murderous plots and a total disregard for astronauts safety.
- Russian Mafia involvement, and the icing on the cake of deceit,
- Boilerplate's testimony.
- Coupled to that are the murders of Hugo Kent and Melanie Illingworth.
- The body parts in the silo bunker

- Gun running

All the above should be enough to bring a government down. Yet nothing is said. The Draper Diaries is labeled as fake. People are saying that the Truth is publishing a hoax about a hoax. In saying this, all these people are acting like indifferent bystanders.

I challenge SEDA and SASS to come clean with the people of the world and expose the failures and crimes of the Athena moon project. Only then will these agonies end. Today friends have been organized to bury our beloved close friend Melanie Illingworth. She leaves a daughter behind, stricken with grief and confusion. Why was Melanie shot when entering a park alongside the brightly lit 5th Avenue? What was the reason? Melanie had no gun or weapon of any kind. She was a passive person, a victim of previous domestic violence. I was there and witnessed the outright murder of Melanie. I saw the murderer gunned down also. I can say this openly, only because I am in hiding and I cannot expose where I am until these matters are properly investigated, and an assurance given, that witness' will not be incarcerated just because they saw what happened.

It is a time of national shame when we reflect on the 50th anniversary of the Moon landing by Draper and Robinson. They, along with Aaron Rosenbach, were murdered, well beyond our jurisdiction. Indeed, well beyond the Earths jurisdiction. One day in the future, humans will return to the moon and find the evidence of these ghastly plots. Until then, let us all hope that someone with the power required, initiates a full inquiry with the authority to access any data need to enable justice to be served."

"RIP Melanie Illingworth You are always Loved and Deeply Missed"

I wasn't holding my breath for a reply or any action against the suspected people. However, I was aware that Cara and I would now be hunted down like wild dogs. And what about Gypsie? There was no way that I was letting her out of my sight. The Warren was not secure and the Ranch was a joke, we had to find a safe house away from this area. Cara suggested Boilerplate's house in Middleton Township. After all, he had been living their passively for nearly 50 years. No-one knows who he really is and neither do we: even though I had an idea. Cara felt sure that he would help. He didn't have a cell phone, so I contacted Belle, who I probably should call Malina at this stage, as Cara was positive about her real identity. She replied with a cell phone number. The old dog! Boilerplate did use modern technology after all.

In the mean time I found that my bank account had been frozen. Great. Thanks for that: you morons. Cara also had no access. But Gypsie did. She had an account in a different name. WTF? This kid is more of a spy than any of the real ones chasing us.

That morning we hired a car with Gypsies credit card and drove to Sandy Hook. It's dumb I know, because that would be out of the way to BP's, off the beaten track if you like. But it was the only way that I was going to remember how to get to BP's house: it didn't appear on Satnav. Even though he hadn't agree yet. Still there was always the creepy silo. I called him and he agreed straight away. So step one was a success.

We arrived and I explained the mess we were in. BP was very understanding and seemed to relate to our situation from experience. There was no problem for the girls staying there. It was a two bedroom mini house really. I could sleep on the sofa. Should have brought my hammock. I had to get back to the Warren to get all my gear and wipe the place down.

On arrival I could see people in the apartment. They must be FBI. I did my commando thing through the looking glass and began grabbing all my notes and backups. Then I heard movement above me. Shit, they will find the door to the basement. Before I could bend down to pick up what I kept dropping they were in the Warren. This is what a rabbit must feel like when a ferret enters his burrow: to eat him.

Loud Voice: 'FBI! You, Kaine stop! Was I going to obey? You gotta be kidden right? I took off as fast as I could still dropping stuff as I ran. It wasn't easy running down there. My shoulders and elbows scraped the walls. Then the bastard fired! The bullets hit the walls and I hit the next turn out of the main corridor, smashing a light as I went. At least in the dark he would have to slow down to be cautious. After-all, they saw me as a cold blooded killer. Reaching the looking glass I wasted no time getting out.

This time there were no commando maneuvers, just me hammering down the street, looking back toward the

Warren. Then more shots. 'FBI. Kaine stop!' I was running so fast I didn't see her. Smash! I ran straight into Malina. Malina: 'No talking just follow!' So I did. I have never run so hard. She was super fit. We got into the back of a sedan as it drove off at full speed. I turned and looked out the rear window and saw Mr. FBI standing there, as other FBIs ran toward him. Fuck that was close.

Malina took me to an apartment in Brighton Beach. Well, I thought, so, she does know the Moscow guys, and they tried to kill me and Cara. Out of the fry pan into the fucking other fire. Me: 'Why are we here? These guys tried to kill me and almost certainly killed Hugo.' Mal: 'Not exactly Mr. Virgil. Yes we are going to meet a Russian, but not mafia.' Well that put me at ease: NOT!

We entered the room almost side by side. I was slightly in the rear ready to run: best to be safe. Voice: 'Hello Mr. Virgil.' What's with this Mr Virgil shit. Well fuck it, it was Khovanski. Me: 'Vasily? What's going on?' KV: 'I just helped a wanted murder suspect escape from the authorities, that's what's going on.' Great, now I would be expected to do his bidding. But what did he want?

At the same time Cara was organizing people to take care of Melanie's body and to see if they could arrange for Gypsie to see her mother one last time. It wasn't going to be easy, as everyone we knew was being watched. Our faces were on TV and in the newsstands. We were wanted murders and child abductors and to further spice it up, Cara was wanted for treason. Can it get any worse?

Gypsie had setup her laptop with BP's Fox cable. She was looking for anything that could tell her why her mother was gunned down in cold blood. She had closed her emotions off and that was a worry. Maybe it was just survival and after the adrenaline ran out she would grieve.

TV Media Release: Breaking News: 'Wanted in the connection with the murder of an FBI agent Teddy Rollins and the cold blooded killing of an innocent woman, are two people. Virgil Kaine and Cara Lucas. Kaine is the publisher of the infamous Draper Diaries and is alleged to have been involved in three murders and illegal hacking of government department computer networks. Cara Lucas is a rogue FBI agent, Kaine's girlfriend and the alleged accomplish in the murders. They are not to be approached. These people are dangerous and desperate. If you see them, call 911 immediately and stay out of sight.'

Great, now we were desperadoes. Anyone in their right mind would rat on us. We were both known, especially me. My photograph was on every column I ever wrote. And now, Cara joined me on a media wanted poster. But they didn't have her short multi colored hair, so that was a bonus. There was a photo of Gypsie from several years ago. Maybe that was to make out we were scum for 'kidnapping' such a cute kid. That's not to say that's she is not cute now.

Back at the park: Khovanski wanted me to handover REV. He said that this is his prime objective. When I asked why, he said that only REV could clear the Russian name and prove that they did not have anything to do with the Athena disaster. It sounded reasonable. But what was I going to say, your REV is most likely dead. Shot by bloody dead Teddy. If I said that I may end up the same way. So I decided to play the game.

Me: 'I am trying to find him myself and after Boilerplate's interview, you should be feeling better about 1967. After-all, he has basically said that SASS killed the astronauts and three other people. Job done wouldn't you say?' KV: 'Yes and no Mr. Virgil. We need all that boilerplate information to be verified. If we don't get it, it is just another hoax rumor.' Me: 'OK, fair enough.' KV: 'You can stay here tonight if you wish or head off to Old Bridge.' Me: 'You know about Old Bridge?' KV: 'Sure. We know your boilerplate and we know who he really is. But that's not up to us to say. He is known to us. We have done some business together. Hmm, once or twice.'

Well that knocked the wind out of my sails and left me in the doldrums and I left Cara and Gypsie there: Jesus! Now there is so much more to consider here. Malina called me over to their cocktail bar and we began a heart to heart. I told her that I knew her name. She wasn't surprised. She said that she was here (meaning in the US) to organize with KV to find Anon: Revenge and pay him handsomely to work for the Russian cause. Which cause, was the question?

She said they were not just about cleaning up the mess from the past. They also want to get a handle on the Moscow Mob, as they are becoming too powerful and their influence is being felt in Russia. Malina: 'Tell Cara that Teddy owed thousands to the mob and was being used by the Moscow to influence investigations away from them.

She shouldn't worry about shooting him. He was a dead man anyway!' Well that made some sense. I didn't ask how she knew it was Cara that pulled the trigger. Here I was, today, chatting with people who may want to kill me tomorrow: isn't life grand.

Cell phone TXT to Gypsie: 'Hey sweetie, could you find me the home address of Rosealee Mishin SEDA director. Gypsie: 'On to it sweetie.' She is a fun kid, and it was pleasing to see some of her humor was coming back, even though I knew it was just a mask to cover her grief. It didn't take her long and she sent the address: it was in Verona.

Back at BPs without questioning about Khovanski because the girls seemed very relaxed. Maybe he had to do some deals to survive. At any rate, later, Cara and I drove to Mishin's house. Bloody big two story mansion on a director's salary. The plan was to enter at the rear and Cara would bypass any alarms. All I had to do was wait for the signal.

I didn't have time to scratch myself and she was in. We weaved our way to the second floor bedroom: guess that's where Mishin would be. The bedroom door was open. I hate that. I can't really sleep with the door open. I stood at the foot of her bed. She was married with no children and good-old hubby was sound asleep beside her. Just as Cara flicked the light switch on, Frank woke up in a startle. Me: 'Stand and deliver!' (I couldn't resist it. I love the old Australian bushranger stories). My right arm outstretched holding a Colt, then Rosealee surfaced. That's probably a bad metaphor in this case. Me: 'Stay where you are. You will not be hurt as long as you shut the fuck up and listen.' Mishin: 'What do YOU! want Kaine?' Me: 'I said shut the fuck up! You are going to end this nightmare that your department began 50 years ago. Too many innocent people are being hurt. Just release the facts. What do you care? You were just a kid then.' Frank was looking at being a hero until Cara: 'Don't temp a desperate woman Frank.'[clue] Her gun pointed directly at his head. Then he changed his tune. I made my point crystal clear. Stop this blood bath and join the fucking human race! Cara tied them up, quite loosely really, so we had some time to get into the next phase of our not so covert operation.

Murder, Gun Powder and Plot

Now we had to get into the SEDA building called Longreach, find the archives department, search for 1967 documents and then find the right ones. That can't be too hard. We approach the building in the early hours of November 5th. Cara managed to kill the alarms. How does she do that? We entered through a back door, just like a real hacktivist but in 3D. Cara had a floor plan that Gypsie received from REV. We followed the mapped-out route. Surprisingly there were no internal alarms and the CCTV cameras where not moving. Something that they would normally do when the motion sensors picked up movement.

Finding the fire door that led to the basement, we went down the concrete stairs into an anteroom. There we could see the locked door that would be our Time Tunnel into the past. Once Cara jiggled the lock we entered and began our search. This was not going to be easy as none of this stuff was stored digitally. It was a case of remembering the old days when libraries had cards and shelf numbers to search with. I guess they still do, but now we use a computer to do the searching.

1-9-6-7 were the numbers we wanted to see, and we found them at the back of this huge room. Still in the dark using a mini LED torch, we both sifted through box after box, until I found a folder with the heading: Information Procedures, Plan B. Of course that could have been something as innocuous as an office filing procedure. However, after taking a quick look, I could see the words Athena. So we were out of there.

The bombing of the Longreach, Verona City, NJ was one of the deadliest acts of homegrown terrorism in US history, resulting in the deaths of 41 people and injuring 200 more, with 96 seriously wounded.

The water truck, packed with nearly 5,000 pounds of TNT and ammonia nitrate, was parked in front of the SEDA building that Wednesday morning, at 8: 30 and was detonated remotely. No-one that we know of bothered to ask questions as to why the truck was parked there for more than 30 minutes. Someone may have, but if so, they surely died in the explosion.

In a matter of seconds, the blast destroyed most of the ten-story concrete building and the surrounding area looked like a war zone. Dozens of cars were incinerated, and more than 100 nearby buildings were damaged.

The FBI was on the job quickly and setup a major task-force of specialists to investigate the bombing. This was a terrorist act, but by whom and why? There were no warnings given. The explosion was planned to take the largest toll of life and create the most damage. The nearby deep space tracking station was severely damaged, and tens of millions of dollars would be needed to replace the sensitive equipment alone.

The lives lost were the greatest of tragedies and the families of the victims were in deep shock. The entire city of Verona was stunned. How could this happen in sleepy Verona, a city of academics and other professionals, with a university tied to the space program. There was no radical movement in Verona. The SEDA building was seen as a monument to American achievements during the Cold War.

Let me state here and now, that Cara and I had nothing to do with this most heinous crime. Being an investigative journalist and Cara an FBI agent (admittedly off the Reservation) doesn't make us terrorists. The news Diaries stating that Cara and I along with 'other' Anonymous activist, planned and executed the bombing is ludicrous. Firstly, I am not considered by the Anonymous world to be one of them, neither is Cara. I am seen as a conduit for their cause. Secondly, these Anons are peaceful people. Sure they will engage in a street protest, but they would never even consider such a horrifying crime as bombing a building full of people.

When the bomb went off, Cara and I were making our way back through the corridors to the exit. Just before the explosion security guards came from nowhere, firing at us. They didn't even say stop. Then the bomb went off and part of the ceiling and one of the walls collapsed. Cara was trapped on the other side of the rubble. She screamed at me to go and called out Gypsie's name. I knew she wanted me to take the data to her. Maybe she was worried that Gypsie was alone with BP, in any case I had to leave. What else could I do? I couldn't move the building rubble there was tons of it. so I couldn't get Cara out. I would have to find another way. I heard her voice, so that means she was alive and most likely would be arrested and held locally.

Outside the air was filled with choking acrid smoke and thick dust. There were chunks of concrete and steel everywhere. How the fuck did I survive that! It wasn't going to be a problem to get away the entire area was in a state of mass chaos. I made my way to the entry car park and tracked overland to a maintenance area, about 200 yards away, where our car was parked. Standing and looking back was a tremendous shock.

Most of the building was gone. How could Cara have survived, and if she did, would they be able to get her out? Would she die from breathing the dust and fumes? Was she alone, or did she end up with those SASS nuts? Questions like that were running a muck throughout my mind.

Then I thought of the other people in the building at the time of the blast. On a full working day, Longreach housed more than 600 people. Among all that carnage there was going to be bodies and body parts. People were standing around in a daze. They were covered in grey dust and their tears, trying to wash dust from their eyes, were trailing over their cheeks leaving a long pinkish line, making them look like the saddest clowns you will ever see. There were local sirens and a huge bank of distant sirens. Screams came from the building, screams of help and screams of pain and fear. I even saw a few tiny dust devils picking their way through the carnage. Pieces of the building were still floating to the ground like weird feathers from some other world. It was the most eerie and surreal scene I could ever have imagined.

This was not only a horrendous tragedy, but hoping you will all forgive me for saying this, but a huge setback for our campaign to expose SEDA and SASS. As it should be, the lives lost here today, will fill the airways and multimedia screens for weeks to come, over-shadowing any other news.

I returned to BPs and gave them the news. Gypsie was beside her self and had some type of panic attack. BP was great with her and managed to calm her down. I hope that rubs off on me so I have those skills when and if I ever become a father. I sat near Gypsie and tried to reassure her that what BP said was right. Cara was a smart cookie and she would be OK. I opened the SEDA folder and un-clipped every page. Laying them out on the floor, Gypsie and I began to look for clues. Hopefully there would be information that would make our mess clean again.

The TV was on and the bombing news was being aired on every channel. The aftermath was horrendous. Dead and wounded everywhere. It looked like some part of Europe during WWII. I couldn't get my mind into gear. I had to go back and trace where Cara was. Maybe Malina would be able to help. Maybe the Moscow gang was responsible for the bombing as a payback for the weapons cache being exposed. Boilerplate didn't think so. He was more inclined to believe SASS had bombed themselves. But why would they kill innocent people. Then BP reminded me that they already had a history of doing that.

I had to hatch a plan to rescue my girl, but on my own it would be fruitless. I needed help so I called Malina's phone but it was down. I rang the consulate asking for Vasily, but he wasn't available. Everyone had gone to ground. So I decided to go to Brighton Beach and ask the Moscow boys for help. Yeah I know that was a monster gamble and probably stupid as well, especially since Cara and I would be prime suspects for the bombing, and the Moscow boys may want my head on a plate, but when a loved one is involved, you will do anything.

BP: 'Virgil if you are going to Brighton Beach I should come with you. The boys know me.' Me: 'How?' BP: 'Well, how do you think I have survived for 50 years without a social security number?' Then he said something that caused Gypsie to release the most important info in this story so far. BP: 'You know we shouldn't disregard the Anonymous as being behind this bombing.' Gypsie: 'Are you mad!' BP: 'No-no. ah, just think, this Revenge fella has all the cards when it comes to computer systems and he could have manipulated the entire mess.' Gypsie: ' REV is not a fella.' BP: 'Well woman then, I don't mind being progressive.' Gypsie: 'No not a woman either. REV is an AI and not responsible for any crime against people.'

So Gypsie had let her cat out of the bag. REV was not a person but a thing. And it must be paining her to think her mother was murdered, by bloody dead Teddy because he thought she was REV. Me: 'Sweetheart, can you contact this AI and get some help in regard to where Cara might be.' Gypsie: 'It's REV, V. and yes I am the only person that REV speaks to.' Me: 'Speaks to?' Gypsie: 'Yeah, We communicate through a Skype type program. I can hear REV's voice and vice versa.' So the hunt was on to find my girl and then rescue her. Gypsie had no problems staying at BPs on her own, so BP and I left for Brooklyn.

How the Mighty have Fallen

BP knew where to go and he took me to a house in Brighton Beach. Brighton Beach is directly adjacent to Sandy Hook across Lower Bay. It is little wonder that the Moscow Mob used the silo bunker to store their weapons cache.

The house was unique for the area. Its roof looked like some type of pagoda. In fact, now that I think of it, it was Japanese in style. Half round roof tiles, quaint rectangular windows and simplistic yet beautiful tall windows rounded at the top. It's a two story house and we entered by the side lane. Inside was opulent to say the least. I could do with this sort of living. But on a jurno's salary, forget it!

BP: 'Здравствуйте. my friends. I have brought you my friend and our guest, Virgil Kaine, from the Truth.' There were seven men in the back kitchen. Some sitting around a table playing a board game and the others watching on. I immediately thought of Bruce Willis, 'three on the left, 6 on the right' or something like that, but where was that guy when you needed him? The biggest man wasn't the boss. I guessed he was the pain.

Man: 'Добро пожаловать Яся, Davno ne bačiliś.' They shook hands and slapped each other's back harder than I would like, but hey, these guys live and die by being tough and they loved to show it. BP: ' Faddei I have to ask you a big favor.' Faddei: ' Разговаривать' do méne русский.' So they had a long chat in Russian while I sat in a rickety chair near the stove literally twiddling my thumbs: nerves can make you look like a complete wanker.

Faddei: 'So Virgil, why should we help you, when you got our guns stolen by USA cops and your bitch is a cop, and she shot two of my men.' Me: ' Because I can get your weapons back, all of them and then offer you the most secret place in New York where you can hide your future products. 'BP: 'I trust him Faddei.' Faddei: 'How we know that you tell truth?' Me: 'I can get Anon Revenge to open doors for you like no one else could. You will be in total control. And when Cara and I return safely to Old Bridge, you will have your guns.'
Faddei: 'We don't like this Revenge man, he has cost us a lot and Teddy was supposed to kill him. But he fucked up. Stupid fuckin' Teddy.' Me: '(yeah stupid fucking dead Teddy) I can assure you Faddei, if I may call you that, that REV will do what I say and you will be left alone once Cara is safe.' Faddei: ' OK Mr. Virgil. We give it a go, Da?' BP: 'That means yes V.' Me: 'Da.' So all I had to do now was get REV to find Cara then call in the mob. What was I doing?

Back at BP's Gypsie had some encouraging news. REV had found nonstandard encrypted traffic running between a country area in Maine and Manhattan. That in itself would not seem strange. But who would be sending encrypted data from the countryside of Maine to Manhattan? Gypsie had traced an IP address to a farming area. We set sail for Maine.

It wasn't long before we found the IP address and its physical location. It was actually in Cumberland, Maine. SASS was working IP addresses through multiple routers to confuse any tracing being done. The house had wooden shingle walls, small grey wood windows and an attached garage made from weather worn split timber. It was surround by a thick wooded area at the rear and a rough weedy lawn at the front. There was a rusty thin pole in the front yard that carried the power line to the house.

BP called the boys and they were not far behind us. When they were in position I parked outside the front and lifted my hood as if I was having car troubles. I sounded the car horn, accidentally on purpose and the front door opened. One guy came over as I was under the hood pretending to know something about cars. Obviously they did not want me there. As he walked toward me the boys went in. They had years of experience doing this sort of thing, robbing people. I felt as if I was now on the side of the fence that I had condemned for years. But hey, I had to save Cara. One of them cut the power line and another grabbed my antagonist and we went inside. The boys had disarmed the goons and were guarding them. Cara was in a bedroom tied to a metal bed. She was covered in dry blood and was unconscious. My fury was evident. I untied her and checked her vital signs. She was breathing but her pulse was weak. I had to get her to Portland ASAP. We couldn't call for an air ambulance but the Moscow Mob has a chopper on standby just in case they had to evacuate their men. BP called it in and Cara and I were on our way. I told BP to hold the fort as I would be back in the morning.

At the Portland hospital Cara was taken to ICU straight away. Then after about 15 minutes, I was still giving insurance details to the hospital admission people when a doctor came out and asked to see me. He said did I know the young woman. I told him our relationship but didn't tell him that Cara was FBI. He said that Cara had multiple fractures of both arms and broken ribs. She also had a fractured skull and had been raped, multiple times. I can't really say how I felt. I remember that my mind went into a haze and he had to shake me a few times and ask if I was OK. I didn't cry. I didn't really say anything for a while. I asked to see her and was led to her bedside. She was sedated so I don't know if she heard me. I bent over, kissed her on the lips and whispered in her right ear: 'I will get them all babe, don't cut out on me please'. A tear rolled off my face and hit her ear. Then I asked them to take care of my girl and left for Cumberland.

I stole a car, because I was broke and in an internal rage. Arriving back at the Cumberland house I found the boys and BP still there. This was my chance for payback. I didn't hesitate. I asked BP for a gun and he handed me a glock. That was good because Cara used a glock. Then I dragged one of the SASS bastards into the bedroom, shut the door. The others were murmuring under their face duct tape, but to no avail. Me: ' I am going to shoot you up the arse you fucking rapist cunt. His eyes widened and sparkled with tears of fear as he quickly shook his head from side to side. I am not proud of what I did, but I had to do it. If I'd left them for the police or even BP's men, I would have felt as if I had abandoned my Cara at Longreach and again here when she needed me the most. And now I needed revenge.

No I was not going to feel that. I pushed the barrel against the bastard's anus and pulled the trigger. He jerked suddenly but wasn't dead. BP had come in on hearing the gun shot and without a pause or any signs of sympathy, put another round in his head.

I stood in the outer room in front of the other SASS rapist. They died in a hail of gun fire from me and the boys. I didn't feel any empathy for them. But it felt strangely good to have done it. Justice for my girl. Later that day I found a quiet place and cried my fucking eyes out.

The Do-Gooder's Wise guy

In quieter days I would count my blessings as a means to start a difficult week. This Monday morning I was about to embark on a mission to recover the very weapons that I had found in the Sandy Hook silo bunker. Weapons that I knew were destined for killing people. I reassured myself that only competing drug lords bought these tools of their trade and so only criminals were killed. But that really doesn't excuse what I am about to get into. For Cara I would fight a pride of lions, but somehow this seemed to be going too far.

Cara was still in hospital and the word was that she had been placed under arrest and a guard was standing by her room 24/7. If I wanted to get her out, I would have to wait until REV could find her medical records and tell Gypsie that she was ready. That was really a long shot. I am putting my trust in a computer program and a mob of desperadoes, keen to kill to get what they want.

BP and I were once more in Brooklyn. Faddei was keen to get his weapons back that day. First I had to find out where they were. SMS from Gypsie: 'Location of products Manheim building, lower basement, in crates on pallets. Manifest to follow.' REV had found them. The Manheim building was in the Bronx, and that meant lots of people and lots of cops. What to do? BP suggested a solution. He thought REV could initiate an emergency at the nuclear power station in Lansing, Tompkins County. That's about 230 miles away. That means choppers and road crews for the NSA and the FBI. Maybe, just maybe, that would leave a window of opportunity, for the boys to get in and out. I told BP to make sure no one gets killed. I didn't want to see a news headline 'BLOOD BATH IN THE BRONX'.

BP was fine with that and Faddei nodded his approval. A message was relayed to Gypsie and onto REV. The reply was, 'give me something hard to do', from the smug computer program. Vehicles were readied and guns loaded. Me; 'No guns!' Faddei: 'Don't worry Mr. Virgil, it is just protection.'

When they left, with BP, I made my way back to Gypsie. I wanted her in plain sight if things went drastically wrong, she was still just a kid. Gypsie and I rested near the TV. News would come in soon and I wanted to get online if I needed to. REV was true to 'his' word and a news report came in saying the Lansing Power Station had a computer problem and evacuations were underway. REV had also sent a ransom message to the FBI. That meant the boys would be on the job in a few minutes. One more news bulletin before I write my next article.

As if running to a movie script, a news flash hit the screen: 'GUN BATTLE IN THE BRONX'. Three armed men were shot by local police as they tried to escape the Manheim building with an unknown cargo. One truck and an unknown number of assailants have escaped.' Just what I fucking didn't want: Jesus, Joseph and bloody Mary, can't they use their imagination to secure the goods?

Faddei got his guns. But at what price? Even though I knew lives meant nothing to these people, and they were not afraid to be imprisoned or to die, a price would be paid for this mobster style robbery in New York. The Mayor was quick to act and called all available NYPD back to duty. The National Guard was on standby for the Bronx, and were already deployed at the power station. I needed to write an article that would reflect the loss of community cohesion, by the reluctance of the authorities to investigate The Draper Diaries. There was an obvious link to the Moscow Mob and somehow I needed to get that across to a wider audience.

Part Three: Adapt or Die

The Pen is Mightier than the Sword

The Truth News Agency had been declared a terrorist organization, can you believe that bull shit, and all our staff were laid off after being interrogated by the FBI. It was no good uploading to the Deep Web, because hardly anyone knew it existed, let alone how to find it. REV came up with a solution. I would upload my articles to his drop box and he would publish them on as many websites as he could. Of course, they would be taken down, but it would take a while and masses of people will be able to read them.

The Truth News Online

August 9 2017

Truth is the Greatest

By Virgil Kaine

"Since I first published parts of The Draper Diaries trouble has been brewing, but to date there has been no investigations mentioned and no rebuttal of Boilerplate's charges against SEDA. Since then the SEDA Headquarters, Longreach, has been bombed and many have died. I am accused of this crime. That is a joke. Yes I was there and yes I ran, but not to escape justice. Rather to bring justice to the victims.

It has been reporteded to me that SASS is responsible for bombing Longreach. I know that sounds just as ridiculous as me being blamed. However, evidence has come to hand that points the finger directly at SASS. They have had an agenda from the very start. Publishing The Draper Diaries scared them into action. They played a dirty part in the Cold War. They have murdered Americans in the name of winning. We have astronauts dead on the moon and three unknowns murdered and dropped from an aircraft.

What does all this mean? It could be that SASS were just caught out in 1967, and didn't have a reasonable plan for the events that happened. So it was easier to kill than to admit defeat. In the long run, SEDA is to blame. SASS reports to the director. However, can an organization as powerful as SASS ever be stopped? What procedures are in place to combat rogue elements? I have not been able to find any documentation that regulates this seriously dangerous public body.

I have put in place methodologies, which will enable others to continue my work. Should I or Cara Lucas end up dead, these plans will be initiated. There is a link between The Draper Diaries and the Moscow Mafia. I might even say, that there is a connection to the Russian Consulate as well. I am prepared to name names and give evidence in a court of law, if I can be assured that Cara Lucas and I are not going to come to any harm. And that includes not rotting away in Guantanamo.

So I waited for any contact through the web. REV hadn't found any messages that pertained to my article. By now I was in a stage of what do I do? I felt totally lost and incapable of defeating the enemy from within. The

Moscow Mob would not be happy with me going against them. But really, did they believe I had turned? I used them to get Cara and now that she was alive and receiving the best medical care (thanks to REV's manipulation of her insurance policy) I had no reason to remain on side with the Mafia. Gypsie and I would have to go. If we stayed here, BP would be in trouble and even may be our executioner. Gypsie and I needed a knew safe house and I had one in mind.

It wasn't so bad in the Presidential Suite. There were beds, bathrooms, coffee, and tea making facilities. The comfort of FDR's secret train was unsurpassed. Yes, I had found a way into the President's underground, and all of the above is false. The train is in a bad state of decay. But we were able to put up my hammocks and clean a space or two. The old carriages are parked near the Waldorf-Astoria platform, originally built for the rich and now used only as a means of escape for a President if required when he is in NYC. We were right under the noses of all the law enforcement agencies and the bloody Moscow Mob. Here we could eat, sleep and continue the fight, safe from prying eyes, handcuffs and guns. It was the first night in weeks that I slept solidly.

The following day we did a rat run through the tunnels to exit in Central Terminal and make our way to local traders, for food and other supplies. I don't know if we were seen. But I had Gypsie leave ahead of me and we met at the food hall on Vanderbilt Avenue. Our next excursion was more relaxed, as both of us had changed our hair and used makeup. Yup! Gypsie insisted that I cover-up that 'sad looking excuse for a face'. With a smile. I barely recognized myself. This time we were after batteries, some cable and tape. We needed another phone aerial.

I took the risk and phoned Malina's contact at the NSA, Antony Webb. I told him that I had all the information he needed to shut down the Moscow Mafia in New York. And that, I would give him this information in its entirety, if he had Cara released to me. And what do you know, the bastard said yes! That gave me a feeling of relief and suspicion. All I had to do now was copy the info he needed to the Cloud and arrange a meet. REV setup the Cloud and Gypsie, always wanting to be involved uploaded all my data. I thought the best place to exchange the URL for my girl was St. Michael's Cemetery Woodside. From there is wasn't far to LaGuardia Airport. REV had setup tickets to Toronto, Canada. But first I had to get some fake passports and the only place I knew was, you guessed it, back in Brighton Beach.

It was a hastily fashioned trip to Brighton Beach. The house I was looking for was on the opposite side to the Moscow Mob, so I felt reasonably OK. This guy I was going to meet wasn't Russian, just a regular incognito John Doe. The passports were going to cost $1500.00 each. Luckily, BP had given me some Moscow finance. So I was using blood money to save us. John Doe had the passport photo images sent to his Twitter account by Gypsie and our IDs to freedom were ready when I arrived. They looked great. I really couldn't pick a fault and hopefully they would be good enough to get us out of the US and into Canada. If that route failed we were all screwed.

Returning to FDRs I called Webb and made the 'meet' tomorrow at midday in the grounds of St. Michael's Cemetery. Strangely enough, I had high hopes that this would work even though all the spy movies show double cross after double cross. Add that to my slight paranoia and you get the picture. The information I had was gold to the authorities and they should be chomping at the bit to get it. Gypsie wanted to ride shotgun. But that was totally unrealistic I didn't want her in sight of Webb, so she would be waiting at the airport.

It was a rough night's sleep in FDR's bed. Gypsie was wandering what the train staff would do when they found out that three little bears minus one had slept in the beds and cooked on the gold leaf cooker. She has a nice sense of humor. In reality, the train is a wreck!

That morning I sent Gypsie off to La Guardia, and I set myself for the most important mission of my life. To recover Cara. I was at the cemetery early, just to check if it was surrounded by agents. It looked peaceful. I guess they are meant to. I watched a black vehicle enter and it stopped just short of where I was. Me: 'Show me Cara!' The rear door opened and there was my girl, looking like death warmed up and in need of more medical help. Webb: 'Do you have the information.' Me: 'Yes. I have it in the Cloud and I've got the URL and password.' That's when I was expecting a big no, but to my surprise he walked over to me. Me: 'Release Cara and I'll give you the information.' Webb: 'I could shoot you now and get that piece of paper and then shoot Cara as well. But don't look so concerned. I will honor our agreement. You and Cara Lucas are nothing to me. I want the Moscow Mob.' Me: 'I am confident that you will and I have certain things in place to protect us.'

He motioned to the vehicle and Cara was helped out. She slowly walked over to me and we embraced: very carefully. She felt so fragile this one time roller derby champion. I had one eye on Webb the whole time. I gave him the paper URL and he turned on his heels and walked back to the car. Was that it? Are we safe? 'Don't stand around looking, go!' my mind told me. Motioning me to stay put, Webb gave the paper to someone in the SUV. Then, after a few moments, a wave from him and they were gone. Was that it? I felt it was too easy. Was I paranoid or was I right?

The data that I released to Webb had every name I knew of in the Moscow organization. The location of their house in Brighton Beach and several other buildings that were used to store illicit items. Those listed included Faddei Danilenko (Moscow kingpin), Malina Georgiou (spy) and Vasily Khovanski (Special Minister, Russian Consulate). REV's investigation had delivered a paper trail that led to a Moscow blind canyon: that made me think of Mel. There were payments made for shipping, something that can't be hidden unless the shipper is a crook. Many bank accounts linked to dubious companies and rentals of warehouses that were known to be used for criminal purposes. The data I gave Webb is all he needed to arrest and detain these people. It would be a very big feather in his cap and I was thinking that is why he is so easy going about Cara's release. We were on our way to LaGuardia and our freedom. I could continue my campaign against SEDA from Toronto.

Southerby

Guy Southerby was a proud career law enforcement officer with the National Security Agency (NSA). He began his career as a West Point graduate. After some time in the military he transferred to the NSA. [Wikipedia] The NSA is a national-level intelligence agency of the United States Department of Defense, under the authority of the Director of National Intelligence. The NSA is responsible for global monitoring, collection, and processing of information and data for foreign intelligence and counterintelligence purposes [clue], specializing in a discipline known as signals intelligence. The NSA is also tasked with the protection of US. communications networks and information systems [clue]. The NSA relies on a variety of measures to accomplish its mission, the majority of which are clandestine.

Originating as a unit to decipher coded communications in World War II, it was officially formed as the NSA by President Harry S. Truman in 1952. Since then, it has become one of the largest US. intelligence organizations in terms of personnel and budget. The NSA currently conducts worldwide mass data collection and has been known to physically bug electronic systems as one method to this end. The NSA has also been alleged to have been behind such attack software as Stuxnet, which severely damaged Iran's nuclear program.

The NSA, alongside the CIA, maintains a physical presence in many countries across the globe; the CIA/NSA joint Special Collection Service (a highly classified intelligence team) inserts eavesdropping devices in high value targets (such as Presidential palaces or embassies). SCS collection tactics allegedly encompass "close surveillance, burglary, wiretapping, [and] breaking and entering".

Unlike the Defense Intelligence Agency (DIA) and the Central Intelligence Agency (CIA), both of which specialize primarily in foreign human espionage, the NSA does not publically conduct human-source intelligence gathering. The NSA is entrusted with providing assistance to, and the coordination of comms surveillance elements for other government organizations - which are prevented by law from engaging in such activities on their own. As part of these responsibilities, the agency has a co-located organization called the Central Security Service (CSS), which facilitates cooperation between the NSA and other US. defense cryptanalysis components.

The NSA's actions have been a matter of political controversy on several occasions, including its spying on anti-Vietnam-war leaders and the agency's participation in economic espionage. In 2013, the NSA had many of its secret surveillance programs revealed to the public by Edward Snowden [clue], a former NSA contractor. According to the leaked documents, the NSA intercepts and stores the communications of over a billion people worldwide, including United States citizens. The documents also revealed the NSA tracks hundreds of millions of people's movements using cellphones metadata.

Internationally, research has pointed to the NSA's ability to surveil the domestic Internet traffic of foreign countries through "boomerang routing". The NSA is currently facing litigation from the Wikimedia Foundation for its potential violation of millions of Americans' constitutional rights, including users of the site Wikipedia, during the government's use of mass collection methods such as Upstream [Wikipedia_4].

These events show how our government miss uses the power we give it. No-one asks can they cross the line, they just do it: whether we like it or not.

We grabbed a bus from West Queens, arriving at the airport. Cara and I met up with Gypsie. Grabbing our luggage we headed for the check-in. There was a public announcement over the speaker system: 'There have been multiple news reports of up to 50 homeless people and squatters taking over the terminals at night and even bathing (naked) in the public restrooms. Do not attempt to sleep here alone. We recommend you to get a hotel room or find an alternative overnight option until the situation improves. Thank you for your cooperation.'

Homelessness was a big problem all over the New York and New Jersey areas. At times I feel we are just goats and the goat herders are the tenant farmers being controlled by the 'Lords' of the land.

As we were moving along the never ending queue, I noticed three security officers eye balling us. Not now surely? We are so close to getting out of this mess and Cara would be at breaking point if she was caught again. They moved closer. I tried to look non plus but that is so hard to do when you are trying to fake it. Should I warn the others? No that would cause them both to look at once and give us away. Security Guard: 'Your ID Sir!' I handed him my fake passport and he checked it out on a hand held scanner. He didn't look pleased. SG: 'Are these too ladies with you?' Me: No, no.' SG: 'Well I require all three of you to follow me, now.'

Shit, shit, shit! What else could we do? It is not easy to escape from LaGardia Airport. We were taken to a secure room and questioned together and then separately. There is no point in me trying to remember what was said. It was just the usual information gathering stuff. If the passports were good enough, then we would be out of there making our meeting with security, just a random check. My main concern was Cara's medical condition. I did tell them to let her go as she was traveling to visit a medical specialist in Toronto.

Then a new player entered the room. He was a typical looking law enforcement guy. Tallish, dark hair graying at the temples. He had a solid build and looked like he could handle himself in a scrap. New Guy: 'Good afternoon Mr. Kaine.' Well that sunk my boat. We were all on false names and he just walked up to me and said my name. NG: 'My name is Guy Southerby and we need to have a little chat.' Well I knew who he was the same Guy Southerby, that hounded poor Hugo and maybe was responsible for his death.

Southerby: 'Look Virgil, can I call you Virgil?' Me: 'Sure you just did. Southerby: 'I need you to help me with the Moscow people.' Me: 'I just gave Webb all he needs so I can't do any more than that.' Southerby: 'Yes you did. But Webb is not playing the game. He is temporary off the Reservation. The ATF has dozens of weapons in that stolen cache and we need to find them before they end up at a crime scene.'

He went on and on a bit but to cut to the chase, I was screwed. He said he wasn't interested in Cara or the girl, especially since Cara had suffered so much. But he could arrest us all for traveling on fake passports. That would be a disaster. So I agreed to listen if he let Cara and 'the girl' go. He did and I had some job convincing them both that I would see them in Toronto soon, and that this was the only way to get them to safety.

Gypsie could see the logic OK, but Cara was blinded by, well fear, and that was so understandable. But sometimes we have to let our emotion go and play the cards that will win the game. So they were out and on the plane. I watched it takeoff and disappear. Now I was beholding to Southerby, a man I quite disliked. He took me to Fort Meade via a fancy chopper. This place was members only. There was no real contact area for the general public just the two buildings surrounded by odds and sods.

Once inside I was taken to a small unremarkable room that had a table in the middle surrounded by a few chairs. No bright lights, no chains or handcuffs, just him and me and a data projector. I was going to watch a video on the Moscow and the gun running business. What Southerby wanted was, for me to publish a few traps online that would hopefully catch some crooks. He couldn't do this himself as Webb hadn't called in the information he got from me. I was beginning to wonder who could be trusted.

The ATF in an effort to shut down the flow of US guns to Mexican drug cartels, began a program called Operation Fast and Furious. On his first day two undercover officers watched a suspected gun trafficker buy semiautomatic rifles at a Phoenix gun store. The agents called in their situation but received an answer instructing them not to arrest the felons. Their instructions were clear: let the guns go. This was the new program of Fast and Furious where agents watched and tracked weapons buyers (also called straw purchasers) to find out where the guns were going and who was involved.

It eventually lead to the death of an agent and the loss of thousands of illegal guns. These weapons ended up with the Mexican drug cartels and were used in illegal killings. Did the ATF allow illegal killing to happen by letting these guns 'walk' to Mexico? And if so who was going to be punished?

The aim of the gun walking program was to break the gun trafficking business not just watch as law breakers were given light sentences by the courts.

Now Southerby wanted to finish the job. The only way he could was to use me and my insider knowledge of the Moscow, to set traps and enable the NSA to complete the mission. The AFT and FBI would be used as ground troops but the command post was definitely Fort Meade. I had told the girls not to contact me. No cell phones no deep web, no anything. I would find them once this was over.

Agent of Influence

One of the problems I was facing was the link between the Moscow gangsters and The Draper Diaries. Of course the Mob, compliments of Boilerplate, had used a secret storage facility under Sandy Hook to stockpile their guns. In doing this, did they know about the burnt remains and the command module heat shield? And why the fuck hadn't Malina given me the test results yet of the samples we took under the silo? And should I tell Southerby about the bodies supposedly buried under the old nuclear weapons silo? If the jigsaw gets anymore pieces I will be at it for an eternity.

My task was to stay at the NSA headquarters until I had published my article. That meant I would need to use REV. And, that worried me, as I would be using the NSA computer system, and these guys know how to move around in cyberspace. Was this a plan to kill off the gun running to Mexico, or to kill off Anon Revenge? And if so, what will become of the 'loose' ends?

I published my article to the Deep Web leaving a request for REV to find it. I knew the NSA was watching every move I made on line. However, what they didn't know was REV was a Cyber AI program. It didn't need to have an address for communications as it monitored the entire web. It knew everything that was going on. As long as a computer device was connected to the internet, REV was watching.

"The Moscow mafia group working out of Brighton Beach have been smuggling guns from the US to Mexico. Many of these weapons have been used in crimes, including murders. The kingpins Faddei Danilenko (Moscow kingpin), Vasily Khovanski (Special Minister, Russian Consulate) and Malina Georgiou (origin and whereabouts unknown) have used the hospitality of this our great nation to turn themselves into billionaires through the collection and laundering of mafia blood money.

Faddei Danilenko the Russian, runs the show and operations out of Brighton beach and is a cold blooded killer. He is an illegal in the US (KGB/SVR operatives infiltrated into a target country without the protection of diplomatic immunity, having assumed new identities and even new ethnicities) and is directly controlled by Vasily Khovanski. Khovanski purports as a special diplomat for the Russian Government, however my sources have told me that he is really the 'New Tarzan' of the Moscow mafia. Khovanski is shadowed by Malina Georgiou, a Russian woman whose father was a Greek citizen. Georgiou is a suspect in the Longreach bombing.

Myself, Cara Lucas, Melanie Ellington and any of the Anonymous that I know of, had absolutely nothing to do with the terrorist attack on Longreach. Moreover, reliable sources have informed me that the security arm of SEDA, SASS, was responsible for the bombing.

The gun walking operations of the ATF, have had mixed success. [CNN]From 2009-2011, under Operation *Fast and Furious*, the Bureau of Alcohol, Tobacco, Firearms and Explosives (ATF) Phoenix Field Division, along with other partners, allowed illegal gun sales, believed to be destined for Mexican drug cartels, in order to track the sellers and purchasers[CNN 2016].

It is estimated that 1,400 recorded weapons disappeared in Mexico. Two of the missing weapons turned up at the Arizona murder scene of United States Border Patrol agent Brian Terry.

The Mob used the Sandy Hook silos as a warehouse until I discovered their weapons cache. Now I can reliably state that they, the Mob, are using the underground rail system used by FDR. Right under the feet of millions of New Yorkers, mafia guns are stored and shipped. One of the biggest crimes in this whole saga has been the ATF allowing weapons to be transported to Mexico, in the vague hope that they can be traced and the buyers neutralized.

Sadly, that could not be further from the truth. Guns are missing. Guns that were recorded by law enforcement agencies have been found at murder scenes. The entire program of gun walking has failed.

The Russian Mafia are well established and have friends in high places who are watching their backs. Locations of houses and storage areas have been passed on to the authorities and a new program is underway to root out these cancers in our societies."

That was it. It may have been my last article or even my last breath. Now I would see what the NSA was going to do. I uploaded two versions. The first I placed in the now defunct Truth server and second I sent into the Deep Web. The Mob was more of a problem than our law enforcement agencies. Sure the NSA could have me locked up for years. But I was guessing that there was more at play here than a moon hoax and some gun running.

Southerby came and got me after I uploaded. He didn't even ask what I said or where I sent it. He knew already I guess. He put me in a car and the driver was going to take me to the airport. Instead he headed for Sandy Hook.

Vasily Khovanski was waiting. Me: 'WTF. Why are you here and where are we going?' Khovanski: 'Mr. Virgil, as you can see, the spy business is a complex one. What you see is often not was is. Just like your space program.' Me: 'So why am I here, are you going to kill me.' Khovanski: Laughing: 'I could have killed you weeks ago, so why would I bother now. You have been working for me, and you never knew it.'

Me: 'So tell me, what are we really doing? What has this whole exercise been about and why did my two friends have to die? He answered as we climbed aboard his speed boat and set sail to God only knows where. Khovanski: 'I will work those questions backwards. Your friend and boss, Hugo Kent, was all most certainly killed by the mafia. That I am sorry for. They saw him as the kingpin. In the Mob, the top man is always considered the main target and the Truth was about to expose their weapons cache. It was only a matter of time before you discovered the silo. Your friend Melanie, she was killed by stupid Teddy as you know because you were there. He was being blackmailed by your Revenge guy. Teddy was passing information on to Malina. You know Malina, right?' Me: 'Yeah sure. So she is a Russian spy?' Khovanski: 'Ask her yourself, she is right behind you.'

I turned around thinking this is when I would cop it, one bullet in the back of the head. But there she was, standing on deck.' Malina: 'Vasily I think he should know before the trip is over.' Oh yeah the trip meaning my life. Khovanski: 'Mr. Virgil, how can I say this? Hmmm. Look there is no space race or moon landing conspiracy. None what so ever. I planted The Draper Diaries for Revenge to find. He had been in the news for some time and we thought it would be more believable if he published the Diaries. We even built the heat shield and burnt pigs flesh into plastic for you to find. Malina did a great job leading her puppy to the food. You see, my benefactors created the entire story. They wanted to shame the USA like it shamed the Soviet Union. All these guys are ex KGB and they don't want to die without payback. All Russians want payback. You see.'

Me: 'So why not just publish the Diaries yourself. And why is the mafia involved? The bay was getting rough. I had to hold on to the rail. Khovanski: 'Forget the Moscow Mob they just happened to be in our way. The gun running thing was to get them arrested so we could continue fucking the USA space program. But now it has, how should I say, misfired. We can continue our plans for payback, but it will have to wait awhile. You see Mr. Virgil, if you had have kept on investigating the moon facts, you would have found out that the Diariess are fake. We did not expect such a dog with a bone attitude from you.'

So they had used fake info to make a fake conspiracy, and in doing so, they had built a well-founded movement that would hound SEDA for decades. Me: 'So now you have told me all this shit, I guess I am fucked.' Khovanski: 'Pretty much Da.' He put his hand into his coat pocket and I headed for the bow. As I pushed passed Malina I pulled her off balance. Khovanski open fire and I leaped into the bay. Bullets zinged around me. I was a champion swimmer at school but I couldn't out swim a speed boat. I wasn't fucking superman!

When I surfaced and turned around I found they had stopped and Khovanski was holding Malina. It looked like she must have worn a bullet that was meant for me. In my hand I had her gun. As I pushed past I pulled the gun from her belt behind her. I took aim and fired ten rapid shots. I was treading water flat out like a lizard drinking. Some rounds must have hit the fuel tank and the drifting speed boat went up like a 4th of July rocket. Bits and bobs flew everywhere and I copped a piece of wood in my shoulder. The shore was only about three kilometers away so I made hast to get there. I ended up west of Brighton Beach soaked to the bone. I took my jacket off and dropped it on the sand. Maybe someone would pick it up before the next tide washed it out into the bay. In my inside zipper pocket was a press card with my name on it. That may be all the authorities need to declare me missing, presumed drowned. So I covered part of the jacket with some clumps of sand. [clue]

After some toing and froing I was back at the Warren. I found my tin of cash I kept just for such an emergency. It was my intention to leave the country as fast as I could. But the best way to do it was via Mexico as the Canadian border would be watched by now and I had no passport. It was a tough ask, as the US border patrol is always on the alert.

On the way I called in at BP's he wasn't home. Yeah it was crazy because he is part of the Moscow Mob. But I had a change of clothes there and I really didn't want to drive to Mexico smelling like a fish. Now Gypsie and Cara would think I was dead. That worried me, because both had been through hell just lately. But I was hoping that my jacket would ring a bell with them as it was sure to be a news item. Think of Yuri, think of Yuri I kept saying to myself, as if the words would somehow make it to Toronto.

Postscript
World News Bulletins
Death Notice September 5th 2017

Today it is my saddest duty to inform everyone associated with The Draper Diaries and all the Truth readers, that the courageous and untiring Virgil Kaine is dead. This is the saddest time since my beautiful mother was gunned down by a crooked cop. I only had a few months to share with my father, and most of the time it was tumultuous. The love of his life Cara Lucas is missing and presumed to have drowned in the East River, after she was seen jumping from the Brooklyn Bridge. Both gave everything to expose the lies and murderous plots of SEDA and their military security wing SASS. I am in no doubt that Virgil Kaine, Truth journalist and Cara Lucas, loyal FBI agent, will in time, be vindicated and therefore proven not guilty of the charges that have been laid against them. My name is Alice. I am Legion. I do not forgive. I do not forget. Expect Me!

Anonymous SMS to Cara: In Mantua.

Local News: Just in.

- ➤ Four decomposing bodies were found in a partially burnt out cabin in Cumberland, Maine today. State Police have said the matter is under investigation and have appealed to anyone who knows anything about the mystery deaths to come forward now.

- ➤ A large piece of what is believed to be, the Santa Maria command module has been found by hikers in rugged country near Mt Katahdin, Maine State police said today. Due to the recent controversy about the Athena mission of 1967, SEDA and the FBI have secure the site. No further information has been forthcoming.

- ➤ Astronomer finds alien spaceship. Joseph McBride an amateur astronomer near Siding Spring Observatory Australia, has recored the optical sighting of a tubular spacecraft orbiting the Sun approximately one million kilometers from Earth. SEDA authorities have said it is just space junk and it is actually in Earth orbit. McBride strongly disagrees and has called on the scientific community to verify his sighting.

- ➤ In other news today . . . .

Fin

References

Coleman, Gabriella (December 10, 2010). "What It's Like to Participate in Anonymous' Actions". The Atlantic.

CNN: http://edition.cnn.com/2013/08/27/world/americas/operation-fast-and-furious-fast-facts/index.html

Kelly, Brian (2012). "Investing in a Centralized Cybersecurity Infrastructure: Why 'Hacktivism' can and should influence cybersecurity reform" (PDF). Boston University Law Review. 92 (5): 1663–1710.

RAAB, SELWYN, (1994) New York Times: http://www.nytimes.com/1994/08/23/nyregion/influx-of-russian-gangsters-troubles-fbi-in-brooklyn.html

Spencer, Luke, 'The Rusted, Rotting Remains of A New Jersey Missile Base' from atlasobscura.com JUNE 11, 2015

Wikipedia:1 https://en.wikipedia.org/wiki/Anonymous

Wikipedia.2 Facts from the Apollo 11 Moon Mission have been edited to suit this fictional story. https://en.wikipeia.org/wiki/Apollo_11

Wikipedia_3:
https://en.wikipedia.org/wiki/Ukrainian_mafia#Moscow_
Mafia

Wikipedia_4   NSA
https://en.wikipedia.org/wiki/National_Security_Agency
Wintzer, Jet, Moon Hoax Now! Full Disclosure 2017